S0-AJF-090

JAKE LOGAN

SLOCUM
AND THE
SHERIFF OF GUADALUPE

JOVE BOOKS, NEW YORK

This is a work of fiction. Names, characters, places, and incidents either are the product of the author's imagination or are used fictitiously, and any resemblance to actual persons living or dead, business establishments, events, or locales is entirely coincidental.

SLOCUM AND THE SHERIFF OF GUADALUPE

A Jove Book / published by arrangement with the author

PRINTING HISTORY
Jove edition / September 2004

Copyright © 2004 by The Berkley Publishing Group.

ISBN: 0-515-13812-6

A JOVE BOOK®
Jove Books are published by The Berkley Publishing Group,
a division of Penguin Group (USA) Inc.,
375 Hudson Street, New York, New York 10014.
JOVE and the "J" design
are trademarks belonging to Penguin Group (USA) Inc.

PRINTED IN THE UNITED STATES OF AMERICA

10 9 8 7 6 5 4 3 2 1

Slocum watched Crane standing in front of the sheriff, who was still seated and calm as ever.

He growled, "Holbrook, I'm going to kill you."

"Anytime you think you're man enough," said the sheriff.

God, Slocum thought, I hope he ain't had too much to drink.

Just then Crane's right hand shot toward the gun at his side, and a roar from Holbrook's Colt filled the air. The shot came from under the table, and Slocum winced with imagined pain as he saw where the bullet hit. Crane, in agony, grabbed at his crotch with his left hand. His right automatically brought out his own weapon and lofted it until it was almost leveled at Holbrook, but he was doubled over with the pain and shock of his grisly wound, and he was looking down at the blood oozing through the fingers of his left hand.

Holbrook brought his own hand from under the table and deliberately fired a second shot, sending brains and blood over the bar behind him. Crane's corpse dropped like a sack of grain.

"Euh," said a cowboy at the bar. "Some of his blood splattered into your beer."

His partner inspected the beer, shrugged, and drank it.

1

Guadalupe was not much of a town, there on the border of Mexico, but it had everything that a fellow needed for a short stopover. There was a hotel, a livery stable, a general store, a butcher shop, a grocer's, two eating establishments, a church and two saloons. There was also a sheriff's office. The hotel was far from full, and the church had only a smattering of folks inside on a Sunday. The stores did enough business to keep themselves open, but the saloons were packed most all the time, both of them. Several ranches were in the area, and they kept the houses of sin hopping twenty-four hours a day. Two of the several ranches were large. The rest were small. The whole place was split by the main road through town. The ranches were on one side, farms on the other. The large ranches were on one side of town. The small ones on the other. It was a lazy place, a good place for a rest.

The two large ranches were the Circle X and the Zig Zag, run by two old warriors who were always almost at each other's throat. It was a peaceful country, sort of. One of the main reasons the two old warriors were not actually involved in open warfare with one another was that they were both busy fighting all the small ranchers. That fighting was not open either, not quite.

Now and then the cowhands who worked for the Circle X or the Zig Zag would get into fights with those who worked for the smaller outfits, when they were all in town having a few drinks. And sometimes someone would catch a small rancher or one of his hands with stolen beef bearing the brand of either Circle X or Zig Zag and there would be a killing. It might be a shooting or a lynching, and there would be complaints filed in the sheriff's office by the small fry, but nothing would come of it. It was expected that cow thieves would be done in. That was the way things were done.

By and large, though, Guadalupe was a peaceful town. Mostly the punchers got drunk and maybe a little rowdy. There might be a fight on a Friday night or a Saturday night, but usually it did not amount to much. The poker games in the saloons were usually quiet, with no one being accused of cheating. The losers just grumbled away from the table to get themselves a consoling drink, if they had the price left in their pockets. Even if they didn't, the winners would usually buy them a drink.

It was a good place to lay around and rest up from a rough time, and it was for that reason that John Slocum had ridden into town. He had left his big Appaloosa at the stable, gotten himself a room in the hotel and was spending most of his time in the Hogback, one of the town's two saloons. He was having a pleasant enough time, not doing anything in particular, minding his own business and staying out of trouble. He had looked at all the whores, but he had not seen anyone who really caught his eye, and he did not typically patronize whores anyway.

Slocum's pockets were full enough for a nice long rest. He had just come away from a job that had paid him well, and he felt like he deserved this long rest. He had been in town long enough to be recognized by most everyone, but he had not made any friends. His acquaintances were all just nodding ones. Everyone liked him well enough, because he left them alone and minded his own business. They left him alone, too.

It was on a Saturday night, and Slocum was sitting alone at a table against the back wall in the Hogback. He had a glass and a bottle of good whiskey on the table. He was quietly sipping the whiskey and casually watching what was going on around him. A young cowhand at the bar was buying a drink for one of the whores, and Slocum silently made a bet with himself that she would be leading him upstairs soon enough.

Suddenly, with no warning, at the other end of the bar, one cowhand slugged another one in the jaw, and the fight was on. Soon there were four cowhands involved. The bartender came up with a shotgun from behind the bar, but he couldn't seem to decide what to do with it. Another cowboy joined in the fray, and then another. Slocum didn't mind, as long as they didn't get too close to his table.

Then the sheriff came in. He pulled his two six-guns and fired two shots into the air. The six combatants all paused to see who was doing the shooting, and the sheriff walked over close to where the fight had been going on.

"All right," he said, "that's enough of that."

"Aw, hell," said a cowpuncher, "there wasn't no harm done."

"Who started it?" the sheriff asked.

The punchers all looked at the floor and shuffled their feet. Finally one of them said, "Damned if I can remember now."

The sheriff put his guns away and turned to the bar. "Give me a whiskey, Amos," he said. The fighters, all tamed down by this, turned back to the bar and bought each other drinks. It had looked for a moment like the Hogback would be all busted up, but it had ended as fast as it started, and no one seemed to remember how it had started. It was a typical Saturday night fight in Guadalupe. Slocum downed the drink in his glass and poured himself another.

He was about to get drunk, and the thought did not bother him at all. He'd had a long, hard fight at his last job, and he felt like he deserved this rest. A little drunkenness was in order and really to be expected. Any man worth his salt would get drunk at a time like this. It was one of life's little pleasures, much to be desired and enjoyed. Slocum felt his last drink go to his head a little, and he decided that he ought to go to the hotel before drinking anymore. He stood up, and he could tell that his legs were a bit wobbly. He grabbed the bottle by its neck and started to make his way toward the front door of the saloon.

About halfway to the front of the room, he stumbled into another man. Stepping back, he said, "Sorry, stranger. I oughta look better where I'm going."

"You sure enough oughta," said the other man, and shoved

Slocum backward. Slocum fell into a sitting position in a luckily vacant chair that happened to be in just the right position. He set his bottle down on the table and stood up. The shove had sobered him some. His legs felt a bit more sturdy under him. The other man took a swing, but he had telegraphed his punch too obviously, and Slocum blocked it and smashed the man in the jaw, sending him back into a table full of poker players.

At the bar, the sheriff turned just in time to see Slocum's punch. The other man was getting up, and the poker players were all complaining vociferously because their game had been ruined. Cards and money were all over the floor. The man stood rubbing his jaw for a moment, then he doubled up his fists, ready to go at it again, but just then the sheriff stepped up behind Slocum with a six-gun in his hand.

"Hold it right there," he said. "All right, partner, I saw the start of this one. Come along with me."

Slocum reached for his bottle, but the sheriff jabbed him in the back with his six-gun. "You heard me," he said.

"What? Me?" said Slocum.

"I told you I saw it," the sheriff said. "There've been too many fights in here lately. They've got to stop. Maybe a night in jail will cool you off."

Slocum thought about protesting. No one from the big fight had gone to jail, and he did not feel as if he had really started this one. He thought about it, but instead, he just said, "Can I take my bottle? It's paid for."

"Hell," said the sheriff, "go ahead."

As Slocum reached for the bottle, the sheriff slipped Slocum's Colt out of the holster from the back. Slocum turned his head quickly to look at the sheriff. Their eyes met for an instant. Then Slocum picked up the bottle and headed for the door, the sheriff right behind him. When he reached the batwing doors, Slocum banged them open as hard as he could. The sheriff was bumped by their backswing and had to fight his way out the door. He was suddenly alert, thinking that Slocum was planning something, but when he untangled himself from the doors, he saw that Slocum was up ahead, walking calmly toward the jail. The sheriff harrumphed and walked along in Slocum's wake.

While the short spat he'd had in the Hogback sobered him

temporarily, the walk to the jailhouse put the wobble back in his legs. By the time they had reached the combination sheriff's office and jailhouse, Slocum staggered against the doorjamb on the way in. He stopped for a moment and looked the place over. Locating the cells, he swaggered over and into one of them, pulling the door shut behind him. He checked the bed and, finding it satisfactory, sat down and tipped up his bottle.

The sheriff opened a desk drawer and dropped Slocum's Colt in. Then he took up a set of keys and walked over to the cell to lock the door. "I'll just leave you here overnight to cool off," the sheriff said. "I'll bring you a breakfast in the morning, and once you've ate, you can have your gun back and go your way."

"It just seems a dirty shame," said Slocum.

"What does?" the sheriff asked.

"Hell, I'm paying for a hotel room, and here I am sleeping in the jail."

He noticed that his speech was slurred.

"I wouldn't worry about that if I were you," said the sheriff. "Just finish your whiskey and then sleep it off. The night'll be gone before you know it."

"Say," Slocum said, "what's your name anyhow?"

"Cyrus Holbrook," the sheriff said. "Why?"

"Oh, no reason. Cy, have a drink with me."

Slocum held the bottle through the bars out toward Cyrus Holbrook. The sheriff eyed him with curiosity. Then he smiled and walked over to take the bottle. He took a good long slug of the whiskey and handed the bottle back to Slocum. He wiped his mouth with his sleeve.

"Thanks," he said. "By the way, what's yours?"

Slocum tipped his bottle up again. Then he said, "What's my what?"

"What's your name?"

"Oh. It's Slocum. John Slocum."

"John Slocum?" said the sheriff. "Say, I've heard of you."

"Oh yeah? What've you heard?"

"Well, let me put it this way," said Holbrook. "From what I've heard, I'm lucky to have locked you up in jail and lived to tell about it."

Slocum handed the bottle back to Holbrook, and Holbrook took another slug.

"I wouldn't place too much stock in them tales," Slocum said. "They get built up some in the telling and retelling."

"I'm taking that into account," Holbrook said.

"Ah."

"Slocum, are you here on a job?"

"A job?"

"Yeah. I mean, has someone hired you to come in here for some reason?"

"I just came here for a rest," Slocum said.

"You sure?"

"Hell, yes."

He handed the bottle back to Holbrook.

"How come you came along with me so quiet like?"

"I don't want no trouble around here. I reckon I can sleep in a jail cell about as well as in a hotel room. I shoulda gone on to my room a little sooner is all. I don't usually get so drunk out in public. It's a fool thing to do."

"How come you started that fight in the Hogback?"

"Oh, you just didn't see the real beginning of it," Slocum said. "That ranny shoved me. Well, I guess I kinda stumbled into him, but I apologized for it."

"You mean he shoved you first? I thought your punch was the thing that started the fight."

"Oh, it don't matter much," said Slocum. "I s'pose you could say a shove started a fight, but on the other hand, you might not think a fight was really started till a punch was throwed. It's all in how you look at it, I reckon."

Holbrook put the key back in the lock and turned it. Then he threw the door wide open. Slocum gave him a curious look.

"You don't need to stay in here tonight," Holbrook said.

Slocum started to walk, but his legs were unsteady. He moved back to the cot and sat down heavily.

"If you don't mind," he said, "I think I'll stay." He held the bottle out again toward Holbrook, who walked into the cell and sat down beside Slocum to take the drink.

"I don't mind a bit," he said. He took a drink and handed

the bottle back. "Slocum, I hope you won't hold this against me when you sober up."

"Naw. It just gave me a chance to get acquainted with you is all," Slocum said. He laughed, and Holbrook joined in the laughter.

"I'll tell you something, Slocum," Holbrook said. "When I saw you hit that fellow back there, I thought about my choices. I figured I had two of them. I could either walk up behind you and poke my six-gun in your back, like I done, or I could walk up behind you and wallop you over the head. I'm sure glad I chose the first of the two."

Slocum threw his arm around the sheriff's shoulders and with his other hand gave the bottle to the sheriff. "Well, Cy," he said, "I'm just as damn glad of that myself."

They both laughed out loud again.

"Slocum," Holbrook said, "you're all right. You know, in a way, I'm glad I arrested you tonight, even if I was wrong."

"Well, by God," said Slocum, "I think I am, too. You ain't so bad for a lawman. I ain't known many that was worth a shit."

"Mostly they're just bad men who ain't never been caught," Holbrook said.

"By God," said Slocum, "I ain't never thought of it that way, but I believe that you hit it just right. Bad men that ain't never been caught. That's a good one. I'll remember that all right. Say, how'd you come to be a lawman then?"

"Aw, it was several years ago right here in Guadalupe. There was some trouble, and no one seemed willing to do anything about it, so I took the job. Just stuck with it after that."

"That's all?"

"That's the whole story."

"Well, by God, I reckon you took care of that trouble all right."

Holbrook laughed a little and said, "Yeah. I guess."

The bottle kept passing from one man to the other, and before long, the sheriff's speech was about as slurred as Slocum's. "Say," he said, "I've got to take a leak. I'll be right back."

The sheriff stood up and nearly fell back on the cot. He caught his balance and headed for the door. Slocum stood up as wobbly as Holbrook and followed him. "Me too," he said.

They made their way through the office and out the back door and eyeballed the outhouse a ways back.

"I'll never make it," Holbrook said, and he turned to face the back wall of the jailhouse. Standing beside the sheriff, Slocum also took his leak against the wall. Done, they headed back toward the door, but Holbrook stumbled and fell.

"Ah, shit," he said.

Slocum reached for Holbrook's hand and helped him to his feet. Arm in arm, they staggered back into the office, and bouncing off both walls, they got themselves back into the cell, where they fell to sitting positions on the cot.

"God damn," said Holbrook.

"You son of a bitch," said Slocum. "I think you got me drunk. Did you do that on purpose or what?"

Both men laughed at that.

"Slocum," said Holbrook, "I can't remember ever having so damn much fun with a bottle of whiskey."

Slocum looked serious and held the bottle out in front of his face and studied it a moment. "By God," he said at last, "I can't either." He took a long drink and handed the bottle to Holbrook. "Kill that son of a bitch, Cy," he said. And Cyrus did. He tossed the bottle in a corner of the cell and stood up. Then he wobbled his way across the small cell to the other cot and fell down on it. Across the tiny room, Slocum fell back, and soon both men were sound asleep, or passed out, in the jail cell.

2

Slocum woke up around seven the next morning. He lay on the cot for a few minutes getting his bearings, letting his eyes get used to being open. Then he sat up slowly on the edge of the bed, testing his head. It was all right. Then he heard a ghastly sound from just across the small cell. He looked quickly, and saw the sheriff lying on the opposite cot snoring loudly. Slocum was awake, and he was feeling all right, just ravenously hungry. A good drunk always did that to him. He recalled that the sheriff had promised him a breakfast, but he did not think that he would get it this morning. He picked his hat up off the floor and put it on his head. Then he stood up and walked out of the cell.

Going over to the sheriff's desk, he opened the drawer and retrieved his Colt, dropping it into the holster that hung at his side. He looked around and found a water jug and a bowl on a table. He poured some water into the bowl and washed his face in it. Pulling a towel from a rack nearby, he dried his face and hands. He walked back to the cell and found Holbrook still snoring contentedly, so he just left him there and walked outside. He aimed himself for Maudie's Hash House, the nearest place to get some breakfast.

Inside, he sat down and ordered coffee. Then he ordered up some ham and eggs, hash browns, biscuits and gravy. He was about halfway through with his meal when the waitress brought the coffeepot around to refill his cup, and he ordered a stack of flapjacks. He noticed a man come in and sit down at the table

9

next to his, but he did not look up from his meal. He was too busy eating. In another few minutes, he leaned back in his chair and shoved the now empty plate away. He picked up his coffee cup. The flapjacks had not yet been delivered to him. The man at the next table stood up and approached him, hat in hand. Slocum looked up.

"Excuse me," said the man.

Slocum eyed him with curiosity, and slowly he recognized the man. It was the same one who had shoved him in the Hogback the night before, the man he would have had a fight with if the sheriff had not interfered.

"What is it?" Slocum said. He braced himself. He was more than slightly aggravated, because he did not want a fight this morning.

"I, uh, don't know if you recollect me or not," the man said.

"It took me a minute, but yeah, I do."

"I just want to apologize for last night," the man said. "I guess I had a little too much to drink."

"That's all right, partner," Slocum said. "I did, too."

"Then there's no hard feelings?"

"Just forget the whole thing." Slocum was pleasantly surprised by the man's attitude.

"Thank you," the man said, and he smiled. "Thank you." He turned and went back to his own chair and table, and the waitress came out bringing Slocum's plate of flapjacks. Soon Slocum was busy again.

When he had at last had his fill, he got up and paid for his meal. Then he walked outside and stood for a minute on the sidewalk sucking in deep lungs full of fresh air. It was a nice day. Too nice, he thought, for ole Holbrook to sleep it away in a jail cell. He grinned and walked back to the jail. The sheriff was still out cold, still snoring loudly. Slocum walked over to the cell and slammed the door with a clank. As the big iron door bounced back open, Holbrook sat up quickly, looking around.

"What the hell's going on?" he said.

Slocum started to laugh, and the sheriff looked at him. Recognition showed slowly on the lawman's face.

"Oh," he said, holding his head with one hand, "I remember

now. God damn it, we tied on one good one last night, I reckon."

"It was all right," said Slocum, "but hell, it wasn't enough to keep you in bed all damn day, was it?"

"Shit. I'da been all right in just a little while."

"What if someone other than me had walked in here," Slocum said, "and found the sheriff sleeping off a big drunk in one of the cells?"

"Well," Holbrook said, slowly standing up, "I might've had a tough time of it come next election, but then, that might've been all right, too."

He walked over to the water bowl and sloshed his face with water. Then he reached for the towel. When his face came out from the towel, he looked at Slocum. "I see you found your Colt all right," he said.

"It wasn't hid too good."

"Let's go get some eats," Holbrook said.

"I've already had some breakfast," said Slocum, "but I'll go along with you and have some more coffee."

They walked right on back to Maudie's and went inside. The same table Slocum had just vacated was still empty, and they sat down there. The man at the next table was still there eating his breakfast. He looked up, surprised to see Slocum again so soon, doubly surprised to see him with the sheriff. He stood up again.

"Sheriff," he said, "there's something I got to tell you."

"Well, go ahead then," Holbrook said.

"Last night," the man said, his voice faltering just a bit, "whenever you took this gentleman over to the jailhouse, well, it shoulda been me you took. I was the one that really started the trouble. I'da told you last night, but I guess I was too drunk to be thinking straight."

"Mister," said Slocum, "I thought I told you just a little while ago to forget it. It's all water under the bridge. Sit down here now and join us."

Almost as soon as the words were out of his mouth, Slocum wondered why he had said that. The man looked back uncertainly at his food on the other table. "Bring it on over," said Slocum. The man picked up his plate and his coffee cup and moved them to Slocum's table. He sat down facing Slocum. Maudie came over to the table.

"More coffee," Slocum said, and Holbrook ordered a breakfast.

"I'll take some more coffee, too," said the third man. Maudie walked off to fill the orders, and as she did, Slocum watched the sway of her full hips. Funny, he thought, that he hadn't noticed her before. She was a good looker all right.

"What's your name, pard?" Slocum asked.

"Me?" said the still nervous man. "I'm Bill Jackson."

"I'm John Slocum, and do you know the sheriff here?"

"We ain't exactly met," said Jackson.

"Well, Jackson, this here is Sheriff Cy Holbrook."

"Howdy," Jackson said.

"Well, don't let your food get cold," said Slocum. Maudie came back bringing coffee all around.

Jackson went back to eating his meal. Through a mouthful of food, he said, "I just wanted to, you know, square things for last night as best I could."

"It's all square, Jackson," Slocum said.

"What do you do around here, Jackson?" asked Holbrook.

"I got me a small spread out south of town," Jackson said. "Hell, I ain't no big cattleman like X. Jones and Sim Yates, but I make me a living all right."

Holbrook put his cup down and glanced at Slocum. "X. Jones owns the Circle X outfit," he said. "Sim Yates is the owner of the Zig Zag."

"Oh," said Slocum.

"They're the two biggest outfits around these parts."

"Seems like I've heard as much," Slocum said.

"You run many cattle, Jackson?" Holbrook asked.

"Just a small herd," Jackson answered. "I got two punchers working for me is all. Most of the time, we just barely hang on, but hell, it's all I got."

"Yeah."

Jackson finished his meal, downed the rest of his coffee and put the cup down. "Well," he said, "I guess I'd ought to be getting along now. If y'all will excuse me—"

"Sure, Jackson," said Slocum. "Stay out of trouble now."

Jackson looked nervous for an instant, then smiled. "Oh," he said. "Yeah. Sure. See you around."

Jackson paid and got out, and Holbrook looked at Slocum. "What was that all about?" he asked.

"Damned if I know," Slocum said.

"I'll bet I do," said the sheriff. "I bet after you had that little trouble in the Hogback last night, I bet that someone who knowed your name went and told him who it was that he tangled with."

"Ah, I don't think—"

"Slocum," said Holbrook, interrupting, "you got yourself a reputation that precedes you. You're going to have to learn to live with that."

Maudie brought Holbrook's meal and a refill of coffee for both men, and the conversation stopped then as the sheriff dug in. Slocum fired up a cigar, puffed at it and sipped at his coffee.

"Say," said Slocum, "who is that little waitress there?"

Holbrook glanced up. "Why, that's Maudie," he said. "She owns this place."

"Maudie, huh?" Slocum mused. He found himself watching her every movement as she bustled around the room. When Holbrook at last finished eating, Slocum said, "How you feeling now?"

"I got me a little bitty headache," said the sheriff, "but that's all. It'll go away here directly."

"I guess that you had a mite more whiskey last night than you're used to," Slocum said.

"I'll admit to being a little out of shape," Holbrook said, "but you give me a chance, I can match you any damn time."

"I'll give you another chance tonight, by God," Slocum said, "if you think you're up to it."

"Well, we'll see. I might have some things I got to do tonight. I ain't a man of leisure like you, you know."

"I know how you sheriffs work," Slocum said. "You don't really have a job. You have a position. You get paid for walking around with that badge on your chest, and every now and then you throw a drunk in jail. Anytime anyone catches you in your office, you fumble around with a stack of papers. That makes folks think you're doing your job."

"You son of a bitch——"

"I've seen it enough times," Slocum said.

"You mighta seen some sheriffs that works like that," said Holbrook, "but that ain't how it is here. Why, just last week——"

"I saw how you handled that brawl last night," Slocum said.

"I didn't see it get started, and no one was hurt, and nothing was broke up. I handled that just right."

"And then you went and arrested me."

"We been over that one already."

"So you don't want to tie on another one with me tonight?"

"I said we'll have to see. That's all I said."

"All right," said Slocum. "We'll see."

"So what're you going to do with yourself for the rest of the day?"

"I don't know," Slocum said. "I came here to rest up for a spell, but it's getting kinda boring around here. In another day or so, I might have to move on down the road."

"Folks're getting to know who you are," the sheriff said.

"Well, it ain't that so much," said Slocum. "It's——"

"You could get yourself in a poker game."

"It's a fool way to lose hard earned money," Slocum said.

"Find yourself a nice little whore."

"I usually don't have to pay for it," said Slocum, and he thought again about Maudie.

"You're a hard man to please," Holbrook said. "Too bad we don't have a public library here for you, so you could entertain yourself proper like. Or maybe an opry house or a ballet theater."

"It'd be all right," Slocum said, "if there was some good company around to go along with it. You know, someone who could sit up a spell and have a few drinks without passing out on me."

"God damn you——"

Slocum finished off his coffee and put the cup down. "Let's get out of here," he said. The sheriff finished his and got up with Slocum. They paid and went out on the sidewalk. "You know," said Slocum, "you still owe me a breakfast."

"What the hell are you talking about?"

"When you threw me in your jail last night, you promised

me a breakfast this morning, but you were too passed out. I couldn't wait for you."

"I guess I did, didn't I?" Holbrook admitted. "Maybe I can talk my way out of it somehow. Let's see. I'da bought your breakfast this morning, but you was in too damn big a hurry."

"No good," Slocum said.

"You never waited for me to release you. You broke out and got your own iron back. I don't have to buy breakfast for no one who breaks outa my jail."

"You told me last night that I was free to go."

"Oh? Yeah, I kinda remember that now. Well, I can't think of nothing else. I reckon I'll have to buy your breakfast tomorrow morning. That means you can't leave until after that."

"I reckon I'll stick around long enough for that."

They looked up to see four riders coming hard into town. One of the riders, a good-looking young woman, was leading a horse. As they drew closer, Slocum and Holbrook could see that the led horse was carrying a body slung across the saddle. Holbrook angled over toward his office, and Slocum followed him. About the time they reached it, the riders pulled up there near them. Holbrook looked up at the man in the lead.

"Who's that?" he asked.

"It's Joe Bob," the man replied. Slocum noticed that the man was not too tall but burly. He wore one six-gun on his right hip and carried a rifle in a saddle scabbard. His hair was white, as was his handlebar mustache, and his skin was red from working out in the hot sun.

Holbrook walked over to the body and lifted the head as if to confirm what he had just been told. "What happened?" he asked.

"Someone shot him," said the leader of the pack. "Shot him in the back, too. Never give him a chance."

"Did anyone see it done?"

"Hell no. You think a skulking back-shooter does his work in front of witnesses?"

"I found him like that out in the pasture," said another of the riders. "When was that?"

"First thing this morning when I rode out to work," the puncher said.

"Was he working alone last night?"

"He was," said the leader again. "Cy, that boy was like a son to me. I want you to find out who done this thing."

"You got any ideas?"

"Hell no. Some of them damn small ranchers. It coulda been any one of them."

"Finding that out's your job," the girl said.

Holbrook ignored her caustic remark and turned to the man who'd discovered the body. "Loy," he said, "you reckon you could ride out with me and show me the place where you found him?"

"Sure," said Loy. "If it's all right with Mr. Yates."

"Yeah," said the burly, mustached man. "Go on ahead. We'll be going down to Riley's."

As the riders, all except Loy, rode on toward Riley's undertaking establishment, Holbrook glanced over at Slocum and said, "You just met Sim Yates of the Zig Zag. This here puncher is Loy. Loy, meet Slocum."

Loy, still sitting in the saddle, touched the brim of his hat.

"Howdy," Slocum said.

"Well, hell, it looks like I've got some real trouble now," said Holbrook.

3

"Loy," said Holbrook, "I'll be with you in a bit. I've got to go get my horse saddled." He started to walk toward the stable, hesitated, turned back to Slocum and said, "Say, why don't you ride along? You ain't got nothing better to do."

"All right," said Slocum, "I will." He followed Holbrook to the stable, and soon both horses were saddled and ready to go. The two men mounted up and headed for the sheriff's office, but Loy saw them coming and rode to meet them. The three riders went together out of town in the direction from which the Zig Zag outfit had ridden in.

They rode a ways in silence. Then Holbrook said to Slocum, "Well, you'll get to see some different country anyhow."

"For what it's worth," Slocum replied.

When they reached the main gate of the Zig Zag, Loy turned in, and the others followed him. The cowpuncher had not said a word the whole ride. He turned his horse off the main road that led to the big house and struck off across country. Holbrook and Slocum rode right behind him. Slocum estimated that they had ridden for an hour and a half when Loy at last halted his horse. A large herd of cattle was milling about.

"Right here," said Loy.

"Exactly?" Holbrook asked.

"He was laying right there," said Loy, pointing to a spot of ground.

Holbrook dismounted and studied the ground. There was a

17

spot which could have been dried blood, and the grass was flattened out some. He turned his head and looked around. A mound of earth covered by a clump of trees rose up off to the right of where they stood. Slocum saw it, too, and he saw that the sheriff was looking in that direction.

"You reckon the shooter was over yonder?" Slocum asked.

"Could be," said Holbrook. He remounted his horse, and the three men rode to the mound. They left their horses at the foot of the rise and hiked to the top. Eyeballing the spot where the body had been found, they began to study the ground. Slocum walked through the trees to the back side of the mound and looked around at the clear ground at the edge of the trees. It didn't take long. He headed back through the trees to the others.

"It looks like a horse was tied back there," he said. "I found some fresh horse shit."

Loy was standing staring toward the spot where he had found the body, but Holbrook was kneeling beside a large cottonwood.

"Yeah?" he said. "Well, I found the place where the bushwhacker shot him from. Look here."

He stood up and held out his hand, palm up. A .45 shell casing was in his palm.

"Looks pretty deliberate, don't it?" said Slocum.

"Premeditated is the word," said Holbrook. "Let's take a look at what you found."

Slocum led the way back to the spot where the horse had been tied. There, close to the fresh dung, they found a low branch which looked like it could have had the reins tied around it, and they could make out the prints of a horse's hooves. They weren't plain enough to distinguish from any other horse's prints, but it was clear that a horse had been tied there.

"Someone rode up here and tied his horse," Holbrook said, "walked through them trees and laid there waiting for his chance. Then he shot poor Joe Bob from behind that cottonwood over there."

"That's sure what it looks like," Slocum agreed.

They walked back down to their horses, and Holbrook looked at Loy.

"Was there any cattle missing?" he asked.

"Not that I could tell," Loy said.

"Thanks for bringing us out here," said Holbrook. "I guess you're through. You can go on back to work. There ain't much more to be learned here."

"Maybe not," said Slocum. "What's the lay of the land here?"

"Huh?" said Holbrook.

"Are we in the middle of Zig Zag or what?"

"Off over yonder," said Loy, pointing beyond the mound, "is the Circle X. The Zig Zag runs way back thataway and for several miles back along the road we come out on. Beyond that is the small spreads."

"What are you getting at, Slocum?" said Holbrook.

"Maybe nothing," said Slocum, and he climbed onto the back of the big Appaloosa. The other two men mounted their horses, and they all rode back the way they had come in. When they got close to the ranch house, Loy waved and headed in that direction. Slocum and Holbrook turned back toward the gate and rode through it and back onto the road that led to town. They loped along in silence for a while. Then Slocum spoke up.

"Cy," he said, "back yonder in town, old Yates said that the shooter was some small rancher, didn't he?"

"There's been trouble between the small ranchers and the two big outfits for some time now," said Holbrook.

"Circle X boys get into fights in town with Zig Zag boys now and then, don't they?"

"Yeah, but it don't amount to much. Both the big outfits is too busy watching the small ones. If they was to get rid of the small ranchers, they might turn on each other, but that don't seem too likely."

"Seems like a long ways for a small rancher to ride to ambush a cowboy," Slocum said. "And the Circle X is just right next door."

"Whoa. Whoa," said Holbrook, hauling back on his reins. Slocum stopped with him and looked at the sheriff. Holbrook stared back at Slocum. Then he started to turn his horse. "Let's ride over there," he said.

The Circle X ranch house was not all that far from the main house of the Zig Zag. The two ranches spread out for miles in opposite directions from the houses. Slocum and Holbrook found themselves riding up to the big front porch of the Circle X in a short while. A tall, white-haired man with a pockmarked face stepped out on the porch as they halted their horses. He had a scowl on his face.

"I was just fixing to ride in to see you, Cy," the man said. "Who's that with you?"

"This is John Slocum, X.," said Holbrook. "Slocum, meet X. Jones."

Slocum touched the brim of his hat and said, "Howdy." Jones nodded.

"What did you want to see me about?" Holbrook asked.

"Someone run off about a hundred head of my cattle last night."

"You sure they ain't just strayed?"

"I'm goddamned sure," said Jones. "And I know where they're at. They're over on the Zig Zag."

"There ain't no fence between the two places is there?" Holbrook asked hypothetically.

"Hell, no, you know that," said Jones. "That's the one thing that me and ole Sim agrees on is fences. We got no use for fucking fences. That's how come we keep riders out over there, to keep the damned critters where they belong. They don't stray over there."

Holbrook dismounted, but Slocum stayed in the saddle. Holbrook walked up closer to the porch and looked up at Jones.

"You have riders out last night?" he asked.

"Damn right. They're out there every night. Mattie and Skunk come in here first thing this morning and told me that they'd heard someone driving them cattle off. They rode after them, but they couldn't catch them. They could tell that they was headed for Zig Zag range though. They didn't want to follow them in there at night. I don't blame them none for that. We're fixing to head over that way and find them and drive them back home. I just wanted to let you know that I'd be riding onto Zig Zag land with some of my boys, but I'm only riding after what's mine."

"You said that Mattie and Skunk didn't want to ride onto Zig Zag range after dark," said Holbrook.

"Hell, no, they didn't. Not right after some Zig Zag punchers had drove off our cattle. They didn't know how many of them there might be. It could be a trick. They could be laying for them over there or something."

"Well, X.," said Holbrook, "someone rode onto Zig Zag range last night."

"What do you mean?"

"Someone rode over there, laid up in some trees, waited his chance and gunned one of Yates's boys."

"What? Killed?"

"Deader'n hell."

"Who was it?"

"It was Joe Bob that was killed," Holbrook said. "I don't suppose you know anything about that?"

"Hell, no, I don't know nothing about it. If it's time for a fight, me and my boys'll be out in the open ready for it. We don't set up ambushes."

"Yeah," Holbrook said. "Well, I'm going back now to see old Sim again, and I reckon he'll say that his boys don't steal cattle either."

Figuring that Yates and his riders had had time to get back to the Zig Zag, Holbrook and Slocum rode back to the ranch house there. They were right. They found Sim Yates at home. Like Jones had done, Yates came out on the porch to meet the riders. The young woman Slocum had noticed in town was with him.

"Well," said Yates, "what did you find?"

"We found an ambush spot for sure," Holbrook said. "It was a premeditated murder. No question about it."

"So what are you going to do now?" said the girl.

"We got some thinking to do, Sim," Holbrook said. "First off, we been thinking about what you said in town. You know, about them small ranchers."

"Who else would it be?" Yates said.

"The place where Joe Bob was killed," Holbrook said, "would have been a hell of a ride for anyone from over there. It was just right at the edge of where your property meets up with Circle X though."

"Are you trying to pin this on the Circle X?" the girl said.

"Now, Josie," said Yates, "just take it easy." He looked back at the sheriff. "It was a good question though."

"I ain't trying to pin it on no one, Sim. I'm just reporting the facts as we've found them so far."

Yates looked at the girl he'd called Josie. He scratched the side of his head and looked back at Holbrook. "Yeah," he said. "That would be a hell of a ride for any of them boys. But they still coulda done it."

"That's the whole point, Sim. The way things look right now, it coulda been anyone. We can't go jumping to conclusions here."

"Well, I guess not."

"And there's something else."

"What's that?"

"We rode over to see ole X. just now," the sheriff said. "He claims he don't know a damn thing about the shooting last night."

"Of course he'd say that," said Josie.

"But he told us something else. He said that someone drove off a hundred head of his cattle last night. Said they drove them over onto your land."

"What?"

"That's bullshit," said Josie.

"Watch your language," Yates snapped. Then he turned on Holbrook again. "But she's right. It is. Why would anyone drive damn Circle X cows onto my range? My own boys sure didn't do it. And no one else would have a reason."

"X. says that he's going to ride over onto your range and get his cattle this morning," Holbrook said.

"By God, he'd better not—"

"Hold on, Sim. I was just going to suggest that we ride over to meet him."

"I'll meet him all right," Yates said. "I'll—"

"We'll all meet him," said the sheriff, "and we'll see if there really are a hundred head of his cattle on your range. We'll see for ourselves. It's like I done said, we can't go jumping to conclusions here. Now, why don't you get saddled up?"

•   •   •

Slocum, Holbrook, Yates, Josie and two Zig Zag cowhands rode across the range to meet up with Jones and his riders. After about two hours of riding, they spotted Jones. Yates spurred his horse, but Holbrook shouted at him and rode out in front. He wanted to stay between the two groups of hostile ranchers. On the other side, Jones and his men had already drawn guns. Holbrook waved at them.

"Put them up, men," he said. "There ain't going to be no gunfighting here today."

Yates and the rest rode up even with Holbrook. "Jones, what the hell are you doing on my ranch?" Yates shouted.

"What the hell are my cattle doing on your ranch?" shouted Jones.

"Shut up, the both of you," shouted the sheriff. "Now, X., you seen any sign of your missing cattle?"

A smirk crossed the face of X. Jones as he turned in his saddle and pointed back behind them. "They're right over there," he said. "We was just fixing to drive them home when you all rode up."

Holbrook turned to Yates. "Sim," he said, "ride over there and take a look."

Everyone waited while Sim Yates rode the distance to the cattle that Jones had indicated. He rode through the small herd studying them carefully. Then he rode slowly back to the side of the sheriff.

"Well?" said Holbrook.

"Well, by God, they are his."

4

A fight between Yates's Zig Zag outfit and Jones's Circle X was avoided, possibly because of the presence of Sheriff Cy Holbrook and Slocum, and all of Jones's cattle were driven back over onto his range. The two small bunches of cowhands, each group headed by its own big boss, separated with no more than grumbles and hard looks, and Slocum and Holbrook headed back toward Guadalupe, after Holbrook had admonished both groups to keep cool heads. Riding slowly toward town, Holbrook said to Slocum, "You sure was quiet the whole damn time."

"Wasn't none of my business," Slocum said. "I just come along for the ride. Remember?"

"Well, all right then," said Holbrook, "there ain't no one around but the two of us now. So what do you think?"

"It could have been one of them small ranchers," said Slocum.

"What?"

"Well, from what you've told me, the Zig Zag and the Circle X have been holding off from having a head-on fight on account of the little ranches."

"That's right."

"It don't seem logical that both big boys would take it in their minds to hit each other at the same time."

"Well—"

"One of them might decide to hit the other one, and then the

24

one what got hit might decide to get back, but it just don't make sense that they'd both take it in mind at the same time with no other provocation. Does it to you?"

"When you put it that way," said Holbrook, "it don't make good sense. But what about the location?"

"I'd say the best way to try to make it look like they was hitting each other would be to pull your stunts over there where the two big ranches come right together. It'd take a little more doing that way, but it might be worth it, if everyone was to fall for it and not think too much about it."

Neither man said anything for at least another two miles. Holbrook pulled out his canteen and took a swig of water. Then he corked it and put it away again. "I think you're right, Slocum," he said at last. "The question is, what the hell do I do about it now?"

"If you're asking me—"

"God damn it. I just did ask you."

"I'd say nothing."

"Nothing?"

"Not a damn thing."

"Yates and Jones is both going to be asking me what the hell I've found out. Hell, cattle's been stole and a man's been killed. Anything might set them off at one another at any time."

"I know all that, Cy," Slocum said, "but what can you do? You got no real evidence of who it was might have been hid in them trees nor of who the hell drove them cattle across the line. The only thing I can think of would be to get them two old men together and tell them what you think. Maybe you could at least keep the peace that way—for a time."

"Yeah," said Holbrook. "Maybe so."

The day was mostly gone by the time Slocum and the sheriff arrived back in Guadalupe. They stopped by the stable and put their horses away, and then they started walking along the sidewalk. They were headed for the Hogback. About halfway there, Holbrook stopped walking.

"Hell, Slocum," he said. "I'd just as well go home and get some sleep."

"You can't take it, huh?"

"What do you mean? Can't take what?"

"I thought you was going to tie one on with me again tonight."

"Well, by God," said Holbrook, "let's go. I'll show your ass who can take it and who can't."

They made their way back to the Hogback, and stopping by the bar, Holbrook demanded a bottle and two glasses. Slocum insisted on paying. They found an unoccupied table and sat down. Holbrook poured both glasses full. Both men drank them down almost at once. Holbrook poured them full again.

"Say," said Slocum, "any of the cowboys in here work for Yates or Jones?"

"There's several," Holbrook said.

"Why don't you send a message out to both men to ride into town tomorrow and meet you at your office?"

"To tell them about your theory?"

"Yeah. It might head off some trouble."

"Good idea," Holbrook said. He looked around the room. "Mac," he yelled out. A cowboy at the bar turned to look. "Come over here," said Holbrook. The cowboy picked up his drink and sauntered over to the table.

"What do you want, Sheriff?" he asked.

"You going back tonight or in the morning?"

"I'll be riding back out to the ranch in a little while," said Mac.

"I want you to take a message out to ole Sim for me," said Holbrook. "Tell him to ride into town in the morning and stop by my office. Will you do that?"

"Sure."

"Tell him to make it about ten o'clock if he can."

"I'll tell him," Mac said. "Is that all?"

"That's all, and thanks."

"Sure thing." Mac walked back to the bar, and Holbrook looked around some more. He spotted another cowhand. He leaned over toward Slocum.

"See that redheaded puncher over there at the table near the far end of the bar?"

Slocum looked. "I see him," he said.

"Go over there and tell him that I want to see him. His name's Bood."

"Bood?"

"That's what they call him."

Slocum shrugged, took a sip of whiskey and stood up. He walked over to the table where Bood was sitting. "Bood?" he said.

The red-haired cowboy looked up ready for a fight. "Who wants to know?" he said.

Slocum said, "Not me. I don't care. The sheriff just asked me to tell you that he'd like to see you over yonder."

Without waiting for a reply, Slocum walked back to his waiting drink and sat down.

"Well?" said Holbrook.

"Well, I told him."

About that time, Bood stood up and started to amble toward the sheriff's table.

"You know," Slocum said, "that's another thing about you lawmen. You get to feeling like anytime you say something, folks ought to jump and run. I've noticed that about all of you."

"Yeah, I reckon we do feel like that," Holbrook said. "And see? Here he comes."

"You want to see me, Sheriff?" said Bood.

"When you going to be back out at the ranch, Bood?"

"Aw, sometime later on tonight, I guess."

"Take a message out to X. for me, would you?"

"Yeah. Sure."

"Tell him that I'd like to see him in my office around ten in the morning. Will you remember that?"

"Nothing to it. Sure, I'll remember. That all?"

"That's it. Thank you."

Bood wandered off, and Holbrook picked up his drink to take a sip. Slocum sipped at his. Holbrook lowered his glass and said, "Well, that's all the business for tonight."

"Well, if that's all the business for tonight," Slocum said, "why don't you pull that tin star off your vest and stick it in your pocket? I can't believe I'm sitting here drinking with a damn sheriff."

"I can't do that, Slocum. Someone might start something in here, and then I'll have to step in. You know how it goes."

"I just don't see how you can relax with that damn thing on you like that."

"Besides," Holbrook said, "what's the difference? A sheriff's just a man back behind the star."

"All the sheriffs I've knowed, it seemed like that star just growed to them."

"It comes off."

"Show me then."

Holbrook looked down at the badge pinned to his vest. He reached over with his right hand and undid it. He held it in front of himself for a moment as if he were studying it, then he dropped it into his pocket. "There," he said. "How's that?"

Slocum raised his drink as if for a toast and smiled. "That's better," he said, and he took a drink. "Now," he added, "take a drink and see if it don't taste better."

Holbrook sipped his whiskey. "It tastes pretty damn good," he said.

"Let's have some more," said Slocum, picking up the bottle to pour. He refilled both glasses. "You know," he said, "a man has got to know how to drink. He's got to be a kind of a artist about it. You know what I mean?"

"Yeah. I think I do."

"There's some men that would fall down drunk or be puking their guts out after a few good stiff drinks, but if you know what you're doing, you can keep right on drinking long after they're all done for and get up the next morning no worse for the wear."

"You're right," Holbrook agreed.

"Say," said Slocum, "tell me about that gal, Josie."

"Josie? You mean the Yates gal?"

"She's the only Josie I've run into around here."

"Hell, you was just asking me about Maudie this morning. You're a fickle son of a bitch."

"No. I'll take either one of them that might be available. I just got to know about them. Is she married? She ain't the old man's wife, is she?"

Holbrook laughed at the thought. "Hell, no," he said. "She's his niece. Her ole man and Sim was brothers. They was partners in the Zig Zag till Isaac—that was Josie's dad—till he died a few years ago. I guess that makes her a partner in the place."

"She got any special men in her life?"

"Not that I know of. She keeps pretty much to herself far as I can tell."

"So far so good," Slocum said. "What about Maudie?"

"What about her?"

"You never told me nothing about her but her name."

"Well, what the hell do you want to know?"

"The same thing. Is she married?"

"She's a widow."

"Is she sparking anyone?"

"She just works all the time. No time for anything else. She must be hoarding up all kinds of money."

Slocum emptied his glass and refilled it. He held the bottle out toward Holbrook, and Holbrook downed his drink. Slocum poured the sheriff's glass full again.

"What about you, Cy?" he said. "You got yourself a gal?"

"Hell no."

"You got to be kidding me."

"Oh, I get me a little now and then from one of the saloon gals, but a man in my line of work ain't got no business getting tied to one woman."

"Hey!"

It was a loud and boisterous voice from up by the bar. Holbrook and Slocum both turned their heads to get a look. Slocum then glanced at Holbrook and thought that he could see recognition on the sheriff's face. The man at the bar had stepped out to stand alone. He was a big man, lanky and tall. His face showed a two-day growth of beard, and his clothes were trail dirty. He wore a Colt slung low on his right hip, and he was looking at Holbrook with an ugly grimace on his face.

"Sheriff Cy Holbrook," the man said. "You remember me?"

"I remember you," said Holbrook. "Lester Crane."

"The last time I was in your town, you walloped me up the side of the head with your damn shooter, and I woke up in your jail. In the morning, you give me back my gun, but it was empty, and you told me to get out of town."

"I'll tell you the same thing again," Holbrook said. "Get out of town, but this time I'll add something."

"What's that?"

"Get out of town—while you can."

"Bullshit," said Crane. "Holbrook, I been thinking about you ever since that time."

"What were you thinking?"

"I been thinking about how good it would make me feel to put a bullet in your gut."

"I wouldn't try it if I were you."

"Stand up, Holbrook."

Slocum slowly pushed his chair back away from the table. Holbrook stayed seated. "Slocum," he said, "stay out of this."

Slocum backed away from the table, his hands held out at his sides.

"That's good advice, mister," said Crane. "Holbrook, I'm going to kill you."

"Anytime you think you're man enough," said the sheriff.

God, Slocum thought, I hope he ain't had too much to drink. Just then Crane's right hand shot toward the gun at his side, and a roar from Holbrook's Colt filled the air. The shot came from under the table, and Slocum winced with imagined pain as he saw where the bullet's path carried it. It looked for all hell like it tore both balls off the man. Crane, in agony, grabbed at his crotch with his left hand. His right automatically brought out his own weapon and lifted it until it was almost leveled at Holbrook, but he was doubled over with the pain and shock of his grisly wound, and he was looking down at the blood oozing through the fingers of his left hand.

Holbrook brought his own hand out from under the table and deliberately fired a second shot. This one tore into Crane's head, sending brains and blood over the bar behind him. Crane's corpse dropped like a sack of grain.

"Euh," said a cowboy at the bar. "Some of his blood splattered into your beer."

His partner picked up the beer and drank it.

"Why, you fucking cannibal," the cowboy said.

Back at his table, Holbrook stood up. He ejected the two empty shells from his Colt and replaced them with bullets. Then he holstered the weapon.

"Some of you boys get him the hell out of here," he said,

and some of the cowboys at the bar immediately obeyed.

"I think you'd better put your badge back on, Sheriff," Slocum said. "And, uh, oh yeah, I see the boys are still jumping when you tell them to do something."

5

A few of the boys did indeed get the body "the hell out of" there, and Holbrook sat back down with a heavy sigh. He picked up his glass and drained it, then grabbed the bottle by the neck and refilled the glass. Slocum strolled back over and sat down. He still had whiskey in his glass.

"That was damn good shooting, Cy," he said.

"Yeah. I killed the son of a bitch, didn't I?"

"Deader'n hell."

"That's the part of this god damned job I don't like, Slocum."

"What?"

"The killing. They don't give you a choice though."

"Oh, you had a choice, all right," Slocum said. "You coulda let the bastard kill you."

"Yeah. I guess I did have a choice at that."

"It ain't a good choice, and you done the right thing."

"Yeah. I guess I did."

"Cy, I never before seen a sheriff or any kind of lawman worrying over a man he killed. Listen, if you'd have made any other choice than what you done, he'd have killed you for sure. Then I'd have killed him. You'd both be dead. Where's the profit in that?"

"There ain't no profit, Slocum. Not ever. Not in this life." He picked up his glass and drained it again. Then he poured it full. Slocum lifted his own glass and sipped at it.

"God damn it, Slocum, you're falling behind," Holbrook said, lifting the bottle. "Drink it on down."

32

"Cy, maybe we oughta lay off for tonight. You ain't in the right mood for drinking."

"The hell I ain't. Go on. Drink it."

Slocum tossed down the remainder of his drink and allowed the sheriff to refill his glass. He could tell that the drinks were having an effect on Holbrook. They would both be staggering out of the place before long. He asked himself what would happen now if another one like Lester Crane should come along. Likely they'd both be killed.

Holbrook was right. Slocum had not kept up with him on the drinks, and Slocum was beginning to feel somewhat woozy. He turned up his glass and emptied it down his gullet.

"Cy," he said, "what do you say we tote this bottle on over to the jailhouse and finish it off there?"

"How come?"

"On accounta if we stay here drinking like this for much longer, I ain't going to be able to walk out of this place on my own. That's how come. What do you say?"

"Hell," said Holbrook. "All right. Bring the bottle." He shoved his chair back, almost pushing it over. Then he lurched to his feet. He tilted forward and had to put his hands on the table to keep from falling. Then slowly he straightened himself up and stood still for a moment getting his bearings. Slocum watched him. He did not want to appear to be as drunk as Holbrook, so he stood very carefully. He felt himself weaving slightly from side to side anyway. He leaned forward to reach for the bottle, and when he did, he too had to steady himself by putting a hand on the table. He straightened himself up, bottle in hand, and looked at Holbrook.

"Let's go," he said.

They headed for the door, Holbrook in the lead, staggering from side to side. Holbrook was just about to push through the batwings when they heard a low voice from the bar saying, "I ain't never saw him like that before." The voice was meant only for the man's neighbor at the bar, but it wafted its way through the thick air of the Hogback until it found the ear of Sheriff Cyrus Holbrook. He stopped, and Slocum nearly ran into him. Slocum slopped to one side as Holbrook stomped over to the bar and grabbed a man there by the shoulder to spin him around.

"Marcus," he said, "there's a hell of a lot you ain't never saw in this life, so you just keep your yap shut about it. If you ain't got nothing better to talk about than how much I'm drinking, go on home and go to bed and jack off."

He shoved the man back to the bar, turned and splattered himself through the door. Out on the sidewalk, his head and shoulders were moving too fast for his feet to keep up with. He grabbed a lamppost to keep himself from falling, and then Slocum caught up with him.

"You all right?"

"Hell yes," the sheriff said.

"Well, I ain't," Slocum said, and he threw an arm around Holbrook's shoulder. "Steady me on over to the jailhouse."

The two men steadied each other, but just barely, as they wobbled their way to the sheriff's office and jail. Holbrook opened the door and they damn near fell into the office. They made it across the floor of the dark room to the near cell and floundered onto one of the cots. Leaning back against the wall, Slocum tilted the bottle back for a drink. Then he handed it to Holbrook.

"I've got to piss," the sheriff said.

Moaning loudly, he fought to his feet and wove his way to the back door. Slocum watched him go through the cell door, but then he lost sight of him. He drank again from the bottle. He heard the back door thrown open. He took another drink, and suddenly he knew that it would have to be his last drink for the night. His head was light and airy. He could easily have let himself fall over on the cot and pass out. He thought that he'd wait for Holbrook though and admit to the sheriff that he had him beat this time. He waited a little while, and Holbrook did not return. Slocum struggled to his feet.

"How much piss can one man hold?" he said out loud.

He fell across the room to the grab onto the bars, managing to keep on his feet. Then he staggered quickly to the far wall. Walking along the wall, he made it to the back door, which was still standing open. Holding the door frame, he looked outside. He saw Holbrook nowhere. He stepped on out and looked around, and at last he found him lying on the ground near a fresh puddle. Slocum staggered over to the body and knelt, nearly falling on his face. He rolled it over.

"Hell, passed out," he said.

He almost let himself fall down beside Holbrook, but even in his fuddled mind, he knew that it would not look good for the sheriff to be found sleeping it off in the alley behind his office. He knew that he could not lift Holbrook, not in his present condition. He positioned himself at the sheriff's head, lifted his shoulders, getting a hand in under each arm, and proceeded to drag him toward the back door. Twice on the way, Slocum fell over backward, but at last he managed to get Holbrook inside. Slocum sat down heavily on the wooden floor and looked over his shoulder toward the cell. It looked to be a long way off.

"To hell with it," he said, and lay back. In no time at all, both men were sound asleep on the floor, with the back door standing wide open.

The next morning, the sheriff bought Slocum's breakfast, and Slocum ate as much as he could hold. They walked back to the sheriff's office by nine-forty-five. "You might as well stay, Slocum," Holbrook said. "You're in on this now."

"I never meant to be," said Slocum. "I feel like I've been conscripted."

"Maybe you have been."

Holbrook built a pot of coffee there in the office, even though both men had drunk their fill at Maudie's with their breakfasts. He was planning to have company soon. At about five minutes before ten, Sim Yates stepped into the office. Josie was right behind him. A couple of cowhands sat in their saddles waiting out at the hitching rail.

"Grab a couple of chairs," Holbrook said.

"What's this all about, Cy?" said Yates.

"You'll know soon enough."

Yates and Josie each found a chair and sat.

"Coffee?" asked Holbrook.

"We didn't come here to visit with you, Sheriff," Josie said.

"I know that, but you're going to be here for a while just the same. Would you like some coffee? It's fresh made."

"I'll have some," Yates said.

"All right," said Josie.

Holbrook poured two cups of coffee and handed one to each of the Yateses. While he was standing there in the middle of the floor, he glanced out at the two riders waiting outside. He walked over to the door and opened it. "You two boys might as well wait over at the Hogback," he called out to them. "We'll be in here for a spell."

Yates turned to call out over his shoulder. "Wait at Maudie's."

The two cowboys rode toward Maudie's, and Holbrook shut the door and went back behind his desk to sit down.

"Now," said Yates, "what's this all about?"

"Just hold your horses a little longer, Sim. I'll fill you in soon enough."

Josie sipped from her cup. "This is pretty fair coffee," she said. "You make it, Cy?"

"Yeah."

"You have any other domestic skills?"

Before he could answer, Holbrook saw the other riders pull up in front. He got up and made his way back to the door to open it. X. Jones was dismounting.

"X., send your boys on over to the Hogback to wait for you. We'll be a little while in here."

Jones looked at the cowboys who had ridden in with him. "Go on, boys," he said. The hands rode off toward the Hogback, and Holbrook stepped inside to one side of the door. Jones walked on in and stopped short.

"What the hell are they doing here?" he asked.

"Shut up and take a chair, X.," said Holbrook.

"I ain't sitting down with Sim Yates."

Yates stood up. "The feeling's mutual. Cy, I'll ask you one more time. What the hell's this all about?"

"Both of you shut up and sit down," said Holbrook. "If you don't, I'll lock you up in the same damn cell."

"On what charge?" said Jones.

"Creating a disturbance," said Holbrook. "Now, sit down."

Yates and Jones glared at each other. Then Yates sat back down. Jones found a chair and sat.

"Cup of coffee, X.?" asked Holbrook.

"If Yates gets coffee, I will, too."

Holbrook poured another cup and handed it to Jones. He walked back to his chair behind the big desk and sat down.

"I asked the both of you to come in here to see me," he said, "'cause I got something to tell you, and I wanted you to hear it at the same time. It looks to me like someone is trying to stir up big trouble, and I want to head it off if it's possible."

"He's already started it," said Jones. "I'm ready for a show-down anytime he wants it."

"I started it?" said Yates. "Why, you double-dealing bastard. You had poor Joe Bob killed. Murdered. Shot in the back."

"Knock it off," shouted Holbrook. "I ain't going to tell you again. Just shut up and listen. Slocum, they got me so damn pissed off I can't talk straight. Why don't you tell them what we figured out?"

Slocum stood up from where he had been sitting quietly and taking it all in. He walked over to the front of the sheriff's desk and sat on the edge. He took a cigar out of his pocket, took out a match and lit it. He took a few puffs to make sure it was going good. "Well, gentlemen, Miss Yates," he said, "me and the sheriff rode out to your range yesterday. You both know that. First we went out to where Joe Bob was killed. We found the place where the shooter laid up waiting for him. There was no real evidence. A forty-five shell and some hoof prints. That's all.

"Then we heard about the rustled cattle. Or strayed. Mr. Jones says they was rustled, and I tend to agree. But it all looks kind of fishy. Both of these things happened right along where your two ranches come together. That makes it look like you done it to each other. But both things happened right about the same time. It come into our heads that if you all was doing these things to each other, you both got the idea at the same time, and we figured that was unlikely."

"Wait a minute," said Jones.

"Just what are you getting at?" asked Yates.

"If Joe Bob had been killed, and that was it," Slocum said, "our suspicions would sure light on the Circle X, on accounta where it happened."

"Well, sure," said Yates. "Them Circle X boys is riding right around there all the damn time."

"Same thing with the cattle," Slocum said. "If Joe Bob hadn't been killed and them cows had been stolen, on accounta where it happened and where they wound up, we'd sure enough have looked toward the Zig Zag."

"Ain't no place else to look," snapped Jones.

"There's got to be," Slocum said. "With both things happening where they did and when they did, the only thing that makes any damn sense at all is that someone else done them both. A third party. Someone that wants you two hotheads to commence shooting at each other."

X. Jones wrinkled up his whole face. "You mean," he said, "that someone else is trying to start a range war betwixt us two?"

"That's the only thing that makes any sense," said Holbrook, standing up and walking around the desk to perch on the corner opposite Slocum. "Think about it. Imagine that you're someone else. Someone with a reason to want a range war started. Sim, where would you go to make it look like X. done something?"

"Why, I reckon I'd go right where poor ole Joe Bob was killed."

"Sure you would," Holbrook said. He turned to face X. Jones. "X., where would you go to make it look like Sim done something?"

"Same thing, I reckon."

"Well, me and Slocum figure it that way. I asked you two to come in here so I could tell you both at one time. So I could tell you that I don't believe either one of you is guilty of either one of them acts, and so I could keep you from fighting with each other. Do you understand?"

Jones stood up slowly. "Yeah," he said. "I get it."

Yates stood and turned to face Jones. He nodded his head. "I'm sorry, X.," he said. "I guess I just kind of flew off the handle."

"So what the hell do we do now?" asked Josie.

Holbrook looked over at Slocum.

"Just keep your eyes and ears open," said Slocum. "Tell all your hands, too. If you see any strangers over yonder where they hadn't ought to be, let us know. If you catch anyone at anything, grab them if you can."

"It's got to be them small ranchers," Jones said. "I knowed we shoulda got together a long time ago to run them outta these parts."

"Hold on, X.," said Holbrook.

"The main thing is don't go jumping to no conclusions without evidence," Slocum said. "You was wrong once. You could be wrong again."

6

The two rival ranchers and their companions had all gone back toward home, leaving Holbrook and Slocum alone in the sheriff's office. For a few moments, they sat in silence. Finally, Holbrook said, "Oh, shit," and opened a desk drawer. He pulled out a bottle and two glasses. "Hair of the dog?" he asked Slocum. Slocum stood up and walked over to the desk.

"Might as well," he said.

"Can't hurt," said Holbrook, as he poured both glasses about halfway up. He put the bottle away and shoved one glass toward Slocum. Then he picked up the other one. Slocum took up his and held it up for a toast. Holbrook responded in kind.

"Cheers," the sheriff said.

They drank the whiskey down fast, like they were taking medicine. Holbrook put the glasses back in the desk drawer. "Now," he said, "we got the two old hogs calmed down some, what are we going to do?"

"We?" said Slocum.

"Well, yeah."

"Cy, just when in the hell did I become involved in this whole mess?"

"Why, damn it, you went out to the scene of the crime with me, didn't you? And you talked to them two old bastards with me, didn't you?"

"I was just passing the time. I'm thinking about moving on from here. I got no stake in this place."

40

"You'd run out on me—just like that?"

"What do you mean run out on you? You got a job here. You get paid to keep the peace and all that stuff. What the hell do I get?"

"The satisfaction of being a good citizen."

"That ain't shit," Slocum said.

"Well, how about this, you sorry son of a bitch? If you refuse to be deputized when I need a posse, I can arrest your sorry ass and throw you in jail."

"You can't be serious."

"Try me."

"Do I get paid?"

"Hell, no. That's just one of the obligations of citizenship."

"No shit?"

"That's right. Well, what do you say?"

"What'd you ask me awhile ago?"

"I said what do we do next?"

"Well, I'd say let's get a big meeting called with all the small ranchers, and let's have us a talk with them."

"All right," said Holbrook, standing up, "let's go then."

They pulled on their hats, walked to the stable and got their horses. In a short time they were riding out of town in the opposite direction from the one that had taken them to the Zig Zag and the Circle X. "The small ranchers are all out this way," said Holbrook. "We'll stop at the first one. Place owned by Charlie Roberts. We'll ask ole Charlie to call the meeting at his place for tomorrow night. How's that sound?"

"Will they all answer his call?" Slocum asked.

"Yeah," said Holbrook. "He's kind a their ringleader, you know?"

It was well past noon by the time they reached Roberts's small ranch. Roberts was not at home, but the door to the small ranch house was opened by Mrs. Roberts—Lizzie, Holbrook called her. She was a rather plain looking woman, not exactly homely, but not particularly attractive, Slocum thought. There were two small children running around the house, but when Holbrook and Slocum went inside, they huddled together behind their mother's skirts.

"When will Charlie be coming back, Lizzie?" Holbrook asked.

"He'd oughta be coming along just any time now, Sheriff," Lizzie said. "He's took young Charlie along with him. They'll be coming right along. Will you set a spell and wait and have some coffee?"

"Why," Holbrook glanced at Slocum, "yes, ma'am. We will. Thank you."

The two men pulled out chairs from the table and sat down. Lizzie poured coffee into two cups and put one in front of each of her guests.

"How come you looking for Charlie, Sheriff?" she asked. "He ain't in some kind a trouble, is he?"

"Oh, no, ma'am," Holbrook said. "We just kinda need his help. We just want to talk to him is all."

"I'm glad he ain't in no trouble. We sure couldn't make it out here without him. No way."

They each had two refills of coffee before the two Charlies showed up. The younger Charlie was about twelve years old. He took off his hat and nodded when he was introduced, but he kept silent. His father also took off his hat. He eyed the sheriff and the other man with suspicion.

"What are you doing here?" he asked.

"We need to talk to you, Charlie," Holbrook said.

"Who's that with you?"

"This here is John Slocum. He's working with me just now."

"Slocum?" said Roberts.

"Howdy, Mr. Roberts," Slocum said.

"Last time someone called me 'mister,' " said Roberts, "he went and stole a horse from me."

"I don't want your horse," Slocum said.

"What is it you want then?"

"Charlie," said Holbrook, "there's trouble brewing between the two big ranches."

"That don't bother me none."

"It should," said Slocum. "Whoever's trying to cause the trouble seems determined to get Jones and Yates at each other's throats."

"What are you talking about?"

Holbrook laid out the situation in some detail to Roberts. When he was done, Roberts said, "And you think that one of us small ranchers is behind it?"

"I never said that, Charlie," said Holbrook. "What I'm doing is two things. I'm trying to stave off trouble if I can, and the other thing is I'm trying to find out just who it is behind all this. What I come to see you about is this. Can you call a ranchers' meeting? Here at your place tomorrow night. All the small ranchers. I want to talk to everyone at the same time."

"And you want me to get them together?"

"I'd appreciate it, Charlie."

"You going to be here?"

"You get a meeting called," said Holbrook, "and I'll be here."

Roberts nodded toward Slocum. "Him?"

"Yeah."

"All right," said Roberts. "They'll be here. Right after supper. Tomorrow night."

"We'll see you then, Charlie," said Holbrook. "Thanks."

Slocum and Holbrook had missed their lunch, so they went to Maudie's when they got back to Guadalupe. When they finished, Slocum suggested that they call it an early night. He was still paying for a hotel room that he had not used for two nights. Holbrook agreed. He went on toward the office and jail, and Slocum walked over to the hotel. Up in his room, he took out a bottle and had a drink. Then he went to bed.

Holbrook reached for his office door and discovered that he had left it unlocked. He shrugged. There was nothing in there for anyone to steal. The extra guns were locked up. He guessed that someone could have come in and drunk up all the whiskey in his desk drawer or looked at all the wanted posters. What the hell? He could have gone on home, but he didn't really want to bother. He would just sleep in the jail.

It was dark inside the office, but since Holbrook was planning on going right to bed, he did not bother lighting a lamp. He took the hat off his head and tossed it on his desk. Then he unbuckled his gunbelt and took it off. He buckled it again and hung it on a peg on the wall. He walked toward the nearest cell and suddenly started. Someone was in there. He blinked his eyes, trying to get used to the darkness.

"Hello, Sheriff," came a sweet but sarcastic voice. "I been waiting for you here for a while."

"Josie?"

"That's right."

"Well, what are you doing here?"

"I come in to talk with you, Sheriff," she said.

Holbrook walked hesitantly toward Josie, just a couple of steps. "Well," he said, "we don't have to sit in a jail cell."

"I like it in here," she said.

"I'll just go light the lamp."

"Don't," she said. "Come on in here and sit down."

"Josie," said Holbrook, moving on into the cell and sitting on the cot opposite her, "what was it you wanted to talk about?"

"I had it all thought out while I was riding in here," she said, "but I can't seem to remember now." She got up and moved across the cell to sit beside Holbrook. "I just think maybe we ought to get a little better acquainted. You and me."

Holbrook turned his head to look Josie in the face. "Josie," he said, "what are you—"

She stopped his mouth with a kiss, pulling his face into hers, parting her lips and snaking out her tongue. In spite of himself, Holbrook responded in kind. She was a lovely girl, and up until this very moment, she had never spoken to him except in sarcastic tones. He put his arms around her and held her tight. Her left arm went around him, but with her right, she reached down between his legs and began to stroke the rise she found there. At last they broke the kiss apart. She nibbled at his earlobe.

"Josie," he said, "are you sure—"

"Sure I'm sure," she said. "Let's get our clothes off and stop wasting time."

Without waiting for a response, she stood up and began stripping off her clothes. Holbrook stood also and began to tear off his own shirt and trousers. He tossed them across the room to the other cot as he did. Soon he was stark naked, and so was Josie. She was sitting on the cot and reaching for him. He started to move down to her, but hesitated.

"Wait a minute," he said. He ran naked to the front door and locked it. Then he ran back to the cell. Josie reached for him again, and this time he moved down on her. As he did, she lay back on the cot and spread her legs. Holbrook moved on top of her, and she reached her arms around him as he pressed his lips once again to hers. With his right hand, he reached down to grip his now swollen cock and felt around between her legs with its hungry head. At last he found the proper place for it, and he thrust down with his pelvis, driving his full length into her waiting depths.

"Ah, yes," she said.

"Oh, Josie."

Josie rocked her hips forward as Holbrook pushed downward, and soon their two bodies were moving together like some well-oiled engine. They humped for several minutes, till Holbrook had to stop to catch his breath.

"What's wrong?" Josie asked him.

"Nothing," he said, "except that I'm getting old."

"I don't think so. Back off for a minute."

Holbrook backed out of her, and she turned over, getting up on her hands and knees and thrusting her bare buttocks at him. He probed again, found her wet hole and shoved himself into her.

"Yeah," she said.

Holbrook bounced himself against her butt again and again, the loud slapping echoing against the walls of the jail cell.

"Oh yeah," said Josie. "Oh yeah. Fuck me, Sheriff. Fuck me hard."

He kept pounding into her, his heavy balls swinging wildly in their sack, bouncing against her thighs. He could feel the powerful pressure building somewhere inside.

"Oh," he said.

"Yeah," she said.

Suddenly he could contain himself no longer. He gushed forth deep inside her, again and again, with each thrust, until the thick come juice was running out of her cunt and down the inside of her thighs. In a few more thrusts, he was spent. He stopped, his rod still embedded in her. He was on his knees on the cot behind her. He gasped for breath. At last, his tool wilted and slipped loose, coming out. It was wet and sticky and dripping. He turned and sat down heavily on the cot, resting his left arm on her bare butt and slapping one of the ample cheeks with his right hand.

"Ow," she said.

She turned to sit beside him, nestling her head against his chest, and he put an arm around her and squeezed her tight.

"Um," she said. "That was good."

"Josie," he said, "what about your uncle?"

"What about him?"

"Does he know where you are?"

"I certainly hope not," she said. "He'd come after you with a shotgun."

"Won't he be missing you?"

"He was asleep when I left."

"You mean you rode in here after dark by yourself?"

"Sure," she said.

"You have to go back tonight?"

"Sometime before morning."

"I can't have you riding around like that by yourself," he said. "I'll ride back with you."

"You don't have to do that."

"But I will, Josie. That's all there is to it."

After they had dressed, Holbrook went to the stable for his horse. Josie had left hers in the alley in back. Together they rode to the Zig Zag. Josie hauled back the reins at the front gate. She looked over at Holbrook.

"You'd better not go any farther," she said. "I'll be all right from here."

"You sure?" he asked.

"Sure," she said. "Say, Sheriff?"

"What, Josie?"

"You ever think about hanging up your badge and going to ranching?"

"Yeah," he said. "I've thought about it."

Josie turned and whipped her horse without another word. Holbrook sat in the saddle and watched as she rode to the corral. In another few minutes, she had unsaddled her horse and was walking toward the house. Holbrook figured that she was all right then. He turned his own mount and started back toward Guadalupe.

7

Slocum found the jail locked up the next morning. He turned and started to walk on to Maudie's, but he changed his mind. Holbrook had walked toward the office and jailhouse last night. He had not walked toward his house. He should be in there. Slocum turned back and rattled the door. When he got no reaction, he knocked. Still no reaction. He walked around to the side of the building and peered in the window of one of the cells. There was Holbrook, all right, sleeping soundly on one of the jail cots. Slocum rapped on the window. Holbrook stirred, but that was all. Slocum thought about going on to breakfast alone and letting the sheriff get his sleep, but then he recalled the way in which Holbrook had conscripted him into staying with him on this damn job. He pounded on the window. At last Holbrook sat up sleepily, rubbing his eyes.

"Hey, you lazy bastard," Slocum called out. "Get up and open the damn door."

Holbrook looked over toward the window and saw Slocum's face staring in at him. He stood up uneasily and staggered toward the front door. Slocum made his way back around to the front of the building just as Holbrook unlatched and opened the door. Slocum stepped in.

"Still asleep, huh?" he said.

"I ain't asleep."

"You were till I beat on the window to wake you up," said Slocum. "Come on and buy my breakfast."

"I bought your damn breakfast yesterday," the sheriff muttered. "I only owed you one breakfast for throwing you in jail. Remember?"

"I figure you owe me breakfast every morning from now till this mess with the ranchers is all straightened out on accounta you conscripted me into working for you and you ain't paying me."

"Well, shit," said Holbrook, leaning over the bowl of water on the table and splashing his face. He straightened up and reached for a towel.

"Well?" said Slocum.

"All right, all right, god damn it."

In a few more minutes, Holbrook was ready, and the two men walked together out of the office and across the street to Maudie's. They found a table and sat down. Maudie was over at their table in a couple of minutes with two cups of coffee.

"Good morning, gents," she said with a smile. "What can I get for you?"

"Steak and eggs," said Slocum. "The sheriff's paying."

Holbrook grimaced at Slocum, then nodded at Maudie. "I'll have bacon and eggs," he said.

"Hash browns, biscuits and gravy?" said Maudie.

"The works," Slocum said.

"Yeah," grumbled Holbrook.

"They'll be right out," Maudie said, and she turned and walked away. Slocum watched her go, noting in particular the sway of her ample hips beneath the slim waistline. Holbrook noticed Slocum's gaze.

"Keep your mind on business," he said.

"I got no business till you tell me what to do," said Slocum. He picked up his coffee cup for a tentative sip. It was damn hot. He put it back down. "We got nothing to do till this evening," he said, "and you got no hold on my thoughts."

The regular breakfast crowd had thinned out some by the time Maudie brought their meals, and by the time they had finished, they were the only ones left in the place. Maudie cleaned off their table and poured some more coffee. They finished the cups without talking much, and Holbrook stood up.

"Let's go," he said.

"I think I'll have another cup of coffee," Slocum said. "You going over to your office?"

"Where else?"

"I'll join you there in a few minutes."

"All right," said the sheriff, still grumbling. He headed for the counter, and Maudie met him there. He paid her and started toward the door. Looking back over his shoulder, he said to Slocum, "I paid for your damn breakfast."

Slocum grinned. Maudie moved back over to his table with the coffeepot and poured him another cup. She was holding another cup in her left hand.

"Thanks," he said.

"Mind if I join you?" she said.

"Why, no," said Slocum. "Not at all. Please sit down."

He half stood as Maudie took a chair and poured herself some coffee. She took a sip and let out a long sigh.

"It's already been a long day," she said, "and there's more to come."

"You're a hardworking woman," said Slocum. "Seven days a week, all day long. Do you ever get any time off to yourself?"

"No, I can't afford it," she said. "It takes all I can do just to keep this place together."

"It's a rough life out here on a woman alone," he said. "I admire you for the way you handle it."

"Thanks."

"You ever think about taking yourself another man?"

"Hell, no," she said. "Oh, I've had offers, but I figure life is tough enough without having to take another man to train."

Slocum laughed at that, and she joined him. He smiled at her. "It's good to see you laugh," he said. "It does something for you."

She put an elbow on the table and her chin in her hand and looked at Slocum with a smile on her face. "Yeah?" she said. "What's it do?"

"Oh, I don't know," he said. "It ain't easy to put into words. It just kind a brightens up your face, I guess. It makes you—"

"What?"

"Well, even prettier than you are normally."

"Thanks, cowboy," she said. "That's the nicest thing that's been said to me in a long time."

"I can't imagine that," he said.

"Thanks again."

Slocum's face colored a bit, and he picked up his coffee and slurped some.

"Slocum?" she said.

"Yes, ma'am?"

"What are you doing here?"

"Oh, I just stopped by for a little rest," he said. "It ain't exactly turning out that way though."

"Why not?"

He told her about how Holbrook had thrown him in jail and all the events that had followed, and then he said, "So he conscripted me."

"He what?"

"Conscripted. You know, like when they take a man in the Army. He just told me that he was making me a deputy or a posse member or something like that, and I didn't have no choice in the matter. So it looks like I'm working for him— with no pay except for when I make him buy my meals."

"Can he do that?"

"He says he can."

"Well, you could go see Burly Baker and ask him," she said.

"Baker? Who's he?"

"He's the only lawyer we got in this town," she said. "He could tell you if Cy can really do that to you. Course, he might charge you for his opinion. They always do."

"They're mostly a bunch of bloodsuckers," Slocum said.

The door opened and a fat, sweaty man with a round, smooth baby face and wearing a three-piece suit stepped in. "Hey, Maudie," he said, "do you reckon I could get me a cup of coffee this morning?"

"Sure thing, Burly," she said. She leaned over close to Slocum and whispered, "Speak of the devil." She stood up to go get a cup. Slocum stood up as well, and Baker moved to the table next to Slocum's and pulled out a chair. He nodded at Slocum as he sat his fat ass down.

"Howdy, friend," he said.

"Howdy," said Slocum. He stopped about halfway to the door and looked back at Maudie, who was on her way to Baker's table with a cup and the coffepot. "Enjoyed visiting with you, ma'am," he said.

"Just call me Maudie," she said. "Till next time."

As Slocum strolled back toward the sheriff's office, he mused about his meeting with Maudie. That next time she mentioned, he thought, could not come too soon for him. Her company was very pleasant indeed, and he looked forward to more of it, much more. He reached the sheriff's office and went inside, finding Holbrook behind his desk shuffling papers.

"It's just like I said. When a sheriff ain't got nothing to do, he pulls out a stack of papers and looks at them. Makes out like he's working."

"Fuck you, Slocum," said Holbrook.

Slocum strolled to the cell where he had found Holbrook sleeping that morning and looked in.

"You have a good night's sleep in here last night?" he asked. Then he noticed something on the opposite cot from where Holbrook had slept. He walked into the cell and picked it up. It was a scarf, a bright red scarf, a lady's scarf. Where had he seen it before? It came to him rather quickly. He had seen it around the neck of the lovely Josie Yates. Holding the scarf out, Slocum stepped into the doorway of the cell and looked at Holbrook.

"I reckon I know why you was sleeping so late this morning," he said.

Holbrook looked up and saw the scarf. He got up quickly from his chair and hurried around the desk and over to Slocum. He snatched the scarf out of Slocum's hand. "Give me that," he said. Then he went back to his chair, opened a desk drawer and put the scarf away, shutting the drawer. "Just forget you ever seen that," he said.

"Aw, come on, Cy," Slocum said. "I'm about the only friend you got anymore. Hell, if you hadn't arrested me, you wouldn't have a friend in the world. Who else you going to talk to?"

"I ain't talking to you or no one else about that."

"What's the matter?" said Slocum. "So you had a woman in here last night. You didn't arrest her, did you?"

"No," snapped Holbrook. "Of course not, you ignorant bastard."

"Well, if you didn't arrest her, then you had her here for some other reason."

"Slocum—"

"It ain't hard to figure out what that reason was. Course, it's kind a surprising, considering the way she'd been talking to you. I guess that's maybe just show for when other folks are around. You know, to cover up for what's really going on."

"Damn it, Slocum—"

"But if she's going to be so secretive about it, she sure ought be more careful where she leaves her scarfs laying around."

"Slocum, if you don't shut up—"

"What are you going to do? Shoot me? Arrest me? Damn you, Cy, you let me carry on about that gal right to your face. Why didn't you tell me to back off then? I wouldn't talk about another man's woman that way, especially if the man's a friend."

Holbrook's tone suddenly changed. He stared down at his desktop and said, "She ain't my woman, Slocum. At least, she wasn't then. Last night was the first time. It surprised the hell out of me. She was here waiting for me when I come in."

Slocum pulled a chair to the front of Holbrook's desk and sat down.

"Hell, up till then," the sheriff went on, "I'da never guessed it. Not in a million years. I always thought that she, well, didn't have no use for me."

"Women will sometimes cover up their true feelings in that way," Slocum said.

"Yeah? Well, I guess so. I was truly just bumfuzzled by the whole thing. I ain't never been took so by surprise. Hell, if she was a man and took me by such surprise, I'd be killed for sure."

"You reckon she'll come again?" Slocum asked.

Holbrook ignored the question. "She had gone and sneaked out of the house after ole Sim was asleep. She rode into town all by her lonesome. I told her I didn't think that was a good idea. Then we— Well, whenever she was ready to go back home, I wouldn't let her ride out there alone again. I saddled up and rode along with her till we come to the main gate. Then

I just set there and watched till she was going into the house."

"So you were up pretty late after all," said Slocum.

"Yeah. I reckon."

"Well, hell, Cy, you don't need to worry none about it. I sure ain't going to say nothing about finding that scarf in there. Far as I'm concerned, I never seen nothing."

"She's a fine lady, Slocum. She's no two-bit whore."

"I know that, Cy. Say, you ain't really falling for her, are you?"

"I don't know. I think maybe I am. That's what's bothering me, Slocum. A man like me's got no business with a fine lady like that. Hell, I don't make much money, and I could get killed just any day. It wouldn't be no kind a life to share with a fine lady like Josie."

It was the first time Josie's name had been mentioned.

"You could maybe go into some other line of work," Slocum said. "That is, if you really want the lady."

"She asked me if I ever thought about being a cow man."

"Well, there you go. She'd likely get you on out at her uncle's place. Hell, it'll likely be hers one of these days. It sounds to me like you ain't got no worries, Cy. Just go for it."

"I don't know."

"You got to get bold, Cy. Hell, she's opened the door for you. Just walk on through."

"Maybe," said Holbrook. "But even if you're right, I got to get this mess with the ranchers straightened out first. That's got to be settled."

"Well, by God, Cy, we'll get it done. We got to get that damn badge offa your chest for good."

8

Tor Stark sat at a table next to the far wall in the Hogback. He sat alone, and he sipped whiskey. He rolled himself a smoke and lit it, taking a deep lungful of smoke and exhaling it slowly, watching the heavy cloud drift up and away. He took a sip from his glass, and then he saw Abel Harrington approaching. As Abel pulled out a chair, Stark heaved a long sigh. "You're late," he said.

"I had a little trouble getting myself started this morning," Abel said. "But what the hell? I'm here, ain't I?" He reached for the bottle. There was a second glass already on the table waiting for him, and he poured it full. "This oughta help," he said. He put the bottle down and lifted the glass for a long drink of the brown liquid. He put the glass down and said, "What's up, Tor?"

"We got us a job to do," Stark said.

"What kind of job?"

Stark leaned forward and kept his voice low. "Rounding up some cattle," he said.

"Where and when?"

"Out at the Circle X," Stark said. "Just as soon as we finish up here."

"In the broad daylight?"

"That's how the boss wants it."

"We gonna move the cattle over onto Zig Zag range like last time?"

"We're gonna move them onto Zig Zag range, all right," Stark said, "but then we're going a little bit farther." He exhaled a cloud of smoke and stubbed his cigarette out in the tray that was provided on the table.

"How's that?" said Abel.

"You know that blind canyon way up on the northern range of the Circle X? Well, we're going to drive the Circle X cows over onto the Zig Zag, and then we're going to drive them north, and when we get on up there, we're taking them back across and into the canyon."

"That don't make no sense," said Abel. "We going to drive them right back onto the Circle X?"

"That's right. That blind canyon is a rough place to handle cows in. Ole X. has had it blocked off by a short piece of fence. He never uses it, and he'll never look for his own damn stole cows in there either. 'Specially if we repair the fence after we run the cows through."

Abel gave a shrug. "Hell, I guess I don't need to understand as long as I get paid."

"You'll get paid all right," said Stark. "The same as always. Let's get moving." Stark picked up the whiskey bottle he had already paid for and carried it with him as he made for the front door. Abel finished off his one glass, got up and followed Stark. Outside at the hitching rail, Stark tucked the bottle into the saddlebags and climbed up on his horse's back. Abel mounted his animal, and the two riders rode easily out of town, in the direction of the two large ranches.

"Cy," said Slocum, "has this town got more than one lawyer?"

"Nope. All we got is ole Burly Baker. I guess that's how come he's piling up so damn much money. Makes me think I shoulda took more schooling."

"Well, hell," Slocum muttered.

"What you asking for?" said the sheriff.

"Oh, nothing much. I just had me a notion about consulting me a lawyer over something, but I met that son of a bitch this morning, and I don't think I like him very much."

"Oh, Burly's all right, I guess, for a lawyer. Them bastards is all alike from what I can tell. They'd sell their own mama's homestead out from under her, take their commission, then beat her out of the profits."

"I believe that," said Slocum.

"You didn't answer my question," Holbrook said. "What the hell do you want with a lawyer? I know something about the law. Maybe I could help you out."

"I don't think so," Slocum said. "Forget it. It ain't important."

"Say, you wasn't thinking about asking for a legal opinion on what I told you about being stuck on my posse, was you?"

"I said forget it. It ain't important."

"It sure ain't. I was right about that. You're stuck, and that's that. Any lawyer would tell you the same thing. Only thing is, he'd charge you for giving you his opinion. That's all. And that's all it would be, too. A damned opinion."

"Fuck you, Sheriff Holbrook," said Slocum.

Tor Stark and Abel Harrington arrived at the place where the Zig Zag and the Circle X came together, the boundary line with no fence. They had made it all the way without being seen. They sat for a long moment looking out onto the range, and they saw no cowhands around. "Let's go," said Stark. They rode onto the land owned by X. Jones. They rode for an hour before they spotted any cattle, but then they saw at least a hundred head grazing contentedly. "Come on," Stark said. "Let's take them." For a time, they worked as hard as honest cowboys, circling the herd, keeping all the cattle together, and at last starting them moving in the direction of the Zig Zag. "Whenever anyone misses this bunch," Harrington yelled at Stark, "it sure won't be hard to track them."

They were moving north on Zig Zag range when Stark spotted a cowboy. At first the cowboy was just looking at them. Likely, thought Stark, he thinks that we're Circle X hands taking some of our cattle back home. They moved closer, and the cowboy started riding toward them. Stark waved, as if everything were all right. The cowboy kept coming. As soon as he thought he had a good shot, Stark pulled his Henry rifle out of the scabbard on the side of his horse and raised it to his shoulder. The cowboy saw what he was doing and pulled up hard, turning his horse. Stark fired, and the cowboy jerked in the saddle. He rode on a little ways, then slipped off the horse's back and fell hard to the ground.

"Tor," Abel yelled from his position across the herd. "Tor, do you think he was alone?"

"Keep your eyes open, Abel," called Stark. "There might could be one more out here with him."

Abel hauled out his own rifle and cranked a shell into the chamber. From then on he was busy keeping the cattle moving along together and watching for any cowhands who might show up. On the other side of the herd, Tor Stark was doing the same thing. They moved along slowly and steadily and warily like that for another twenty minutes or so before Harrington spotted the second cowboy. He was dead ahead. The shot would have been about the same for either Harrington or Stark. Harrington raised his rifle, but the cowboy turned and rode hard, heading back toward the ranch house.

"Tor," Abel called out.

"Stop him," yelled Stark.

Both men rode hard after the cowboy, abandoning the herd of stolen cattle. The cowboy topped a rise and disappeared from view, but the two outlaws kept riding hard. They reached the top of the rise and spotted him again. The distance was still great between them, but as Stark continued in pursuit, Harrington stopped his horse and dismounted. He flopped himself on the ground and took careful aim. He fired, and smiled as he saw the cowboy drop from the saddle. Stark kept riding. When he reached the fallen cowboy, he stopped and looked down at the body with the gaping hole in its back. He turned and rode back to his partner.

"That was a good shot, Abel," he said.

Harrington was just settling down in his saddle again. He looked at Stark and smiled. "I can usually make them like that, if I settle down real good first."

"Let's get back to them cows," said Stark.

It was well into the afternoon, and Slocum and Holbrook were riding toward the meeting of the small ranchers at the Roberts spread. They had been riding in silence for a ways, when Slocum at last spoke. "Cy," he said, "just what the hell is it we're supposed to be accomplishing by this damn meeting?"

"Hell, I done told you that."

"Well, tell me again, damn it."

"All right, Slocum," Holbrook said. "We're going to make sure that all the ranchers is there, first off. Then, just in case we're wrong about what's going on, we're going to kinda size them up, you know."

"What the hell can you tell about a man by sizing him up?"

"You can tell a lot," said Holbrook. "Damn it. Finally, we're going to tell them all the same things what we told the big boys. To keep their heads cool. That we suspect that some third party might could be behind all this, and we don't want no one jumping the gun on us. We don't want a damn range war to get started whether it's between Jones and Yates or it's Jones and Yates together against the small ranches. You get it?"

"I got it," said Slocum.

When they arrived at Roberts's house, it was obvious from the number of horses, wagons and buggies around the place that most everyone was there. They dismounted and hitched their horses. As they walked toward the house, young Charlie met them.

"They're all inside waiting for you," he said, and he led the way to the house and opened the door. Holbrook and Slocum followed him in.

"Howdy, Sheriff," said the older Charlie Roberts. "Slocum."

"You got them all here?" Holbrook asked.

"Every damn one," said Roberts.

"Good," Holbrook said. "We might as well get started and not waste any more of anyone's time than we have to."

Roberts called for attention, and Holbrook stepped forward. Everyone stopped what he was doing to pay attention. They had some inkling of what the sheriff was up to, but no one was totally certain, and everyone was curious. Holbrook started out by introducing Slocum as his deputy, and Slocum scowled at the thought. Then the sheriff told the crowd about the trouble on the two big ranches. The reaction was about what he expected, about the same as he had initially received from Charlie

Roberts. He let them laugh and sneer for a short while. Then he calmed them down again.

"I know that none of you got no love for ole X. Jones, nor any for Sim Yates neither," he said. "But I'm here to tell you that if serious trouble gets started up between them, you're all going to be drawn into it, like it or not."

He went on to explain to them how both ranchers had at first blamed each other and were ready to ride over with guns blazing. He told them how he and Slocum had managed to hold them back and explain their theory to them and at least seem to convince them.

"You see," Holbrook said, "what we believe is that a third party, as yet unknown, is at the bottom of all this. I don't know what it is he wants, but it's pretty damn obvious that he wants trouble between the two big ranchers and to blame it on you boys."

"Sheriff," said one of the men gathered there, "how come would somebody want to see us in a big fight?"

"I can't answer that, Zeke," said Holbrook, glancing toward Slocum. "Not till I know who it is behind all this."

Slocum had been leaning on the back wall. He straightened up and took a few steps forward.

"It could be a couple of things," he said, "and it might help if you boys was to think about them for a while. If a range war was to get started, there'd be a winner and a loser. The winner would be weaker than he was whenever it started. The loser might not even still be around. In this case here there's three of you involved. I have an idea that whoever the loser would be, as soon as it was all said and done, the war would start up again between the two that was left. After two wars, the winner would be considerable weakened. One way to figure it all out would be to just wait it out and let the wars start. When it's all over with, we'll know who was behind it, but it will be too late then."

Charlie Roberts came forward then. "All right," he said. "What is it we think about?"

"Who might want you men out of business? Who might want your range? Same with the big boys. Who'd want them out of the way?"

"That's easy," said an old-timer in the crowd. "We want the

Zig Zag and the Circle X shut down, and the Circle X and the Zig Zag wants us out of here."

"You're right," Slocum said, "but it's too easy. You got to think beyond that, 'cause whoever this is wants all of you out of here. You got to go beyond your old feuds with Yates and Jones. There's someone else in this fight, and it's someone you ain't thought about yet."

"Someone else," someone muttered.

"Who the hell could it be?"

Lizzie Roberts took advantage of the lull in the meeting to offer coffee all around. Slocum thanked her and took a cup. Most everyone did. Finally Holbrook tried to get control of the meeting again. Roberts saw what he was doing and got up to help. Slowly the crowd quieted down.

"I'm going to tell you all just how I'm looking at this thing right now," the sheriff said. "I'm thinking that the one we're looking for could be anyone. Now, I don't believe that it's you boys. Someone's trying to make it look that a way is all. At least, I don't believe that it's you boys as a bunch."

"What do you mean by that?" said the old-timer.

"I mean that it could be any one of you acting on his own. Someone in the group who's madder than the others for whatever reason."

The crowd grew boisterous again, and Holbrook and Roberts had a time getting them to quiet down this time. At last they did, and Holbrook went on.

"I didn't say that it was one of you," he said. "All I said is that I got to think like that. It could be one of you. Then again, it could be one of Sim Yates's cowboys or one of X. Jones's. Then again, it might be someone in town."

"Or someone out of town who's hired someone to do his dirty work," said the old-timer.

"It could be," said Holbrook.

Slocum stepped up again. "Keep your eyes on strangers," he said. "If you see anyone or anything suspicious, report it to the sheriff. The main thing is—don't start no shooting. Don't shoot at anyone unless he shoots first."

•   •   •

Riding back toward Guadalupe, Holbrook asked Slocum, "How do you think our meeting went?"

Slocum shrugged. "We said what we went out there to say."

"Well, I think the boys took it all pretty well," Holbrook said. "I think they understood all right."

"They understood us," said Slocum. "That don't mean that they'll do what we asked them to do. Watch the saloons. See if there's any fights started, and see who starts them. See if there's any more shooting. It'll take a few days before we find out if they really listened."

"Yeah," said Holbrook. "I reckon."

"If it takes us much longer than that to figure this thing out," Slocum said, "it won't much matter."

"What do you mean?"

"They'll all be trying to kill everyone else."

9

Early the next morning Sim Yates was at the sheriff's office with four cowhands and Josie when Holbrook and Slocum got back from breakfast. Their horses were at the hitching rail, and the riders were all lounging sullenly around on the sidewalk. Holbrook stepped up among them, while Slocum remained in the street.

"What's this all about?" the sheriff asked.

"Two more of my boys was killed last night," Yates said.

"My God," said Holbrook. "Any witnesses?"

"Only them that's dead."

Holbrook unlocked his office door and went inside slowly. He moved behind his desk, sat down and put his head in his hands. Yates and the others followed him in, and Slocum waited and moved in last.

"Cy," said Yates, "I understand your theory about what's going on here, but understanding is one thing. Putting up with cowhands getting murdered every few days is something else. What the hell are you going to do?"

"God damn it, Sim, I don't know," said Holbrook. "Me and Slocum went out last night to Roberts's place for a meeting of all the small ranchers. We give them our thoughts on all this, and they agreed to hold off. I don't know what else we can do. You men need to double up on your guards. That's all I can think of. Slocum?"

Holbrook's voice sounded desperate, and Slocum felt for

him. He understood the frustration the sheriff must have been feeling. He had nothing more to add though. Not really. He gave a shrug.

"All I can think of is to tell you what we told them last night. Be thinking of anyone you can who might profit from shutting you all down. Someone's doing all this for a reason."

"Jones has wanted to shut me down for years," Yates said, "and all them squatters."

"I don't believe it's either one of them," Slocum said.

"Well, you better come up with something real damn soon," Yates said. He turned and stomped out of the office, and the four cowboys followed him. Josie lingered behind. She stood for a moment in silence, looking at Holbrook. At last she spoke.

"I know you're trying, Cy," she said, "and I know it's not easy. I only hope you can come up with something before it's too late." She followed the others out. They all mounted up and rode back out of town. Holbrook looked at Slocum with a helpless expression on his face.

"Well," he said, "let's ride out there."

They rode first to the Circle X, where they found Jones having a horse saddled, with a half dozen men around him. Holbrook and Slocum rode over to the corral and stopped.

"What's going on, X.?" Holbrook asked.

"About a hundred head was stole last night," said Jones. "That's what. We're riding out now to look over the land. You want to ride along?"

"We'll join you," said Holbrook. "When I went to the office this morning, Sim Yates was waiting for me. He had two more of his boys killed last night."

"What?"

"Yeah."

"I'll be god damned."

"It looks to me like the same plan we talked about before," Slocum said. "Someone rode out here sometime yesterday and killed two of the Zig Zag riders and then apparently run off some of your cattle."

"We've already been out to the road," Jones said. "No cattle has been drove out that way."

"And there ain't no other way," said Holbrook, "except on your land or Yates's."

"That's exactly right," Jones said. The cowboy who was saddling the old man's horse stepped aside, indicating that he was done, and Jones climbed laboriously up onto the horse's back. "Let's ride," he said.

In a while they reached the area where the missing cattle were last known to be. It did not take long to read the indications that the animals had been driven straight over to the Zig Zag.

"I know what you said, Cy," Jones said, "but this is hard to take."

"Don't jump to no conclusions, X.," Holbrook said. "Let's follow the trail."

They rode onto the Zig Zag and met up with a couple of Yates's cowboys. Holbrook hailed them quickly, so they would know that he was along. The cowboys rode on over to meet Holbrook, Slocum and the Circle X bunch. Slocum recognized Loy and Mac.

"What are you all up to?" Loy asked.

"We're tracking some stole cattle," said Jones. "That's what. You can read them tracks, can't you?"

Loy and Mac rode around a bit studying the ground. Then Loy rode back over to where old Jones sat in his saddle. "Looks like someone drove some of yours over here again," he said.

"Looks like, don't it?" Jones said.

"What are you boys doing over here?" Holbrook asked.

"It was round about here that our boys was killed yesterday," he said. "The boss sent us out to look over the land."

"Slocum," said Holbrook, "I'll ride on with Jones. Why don't you hang around with Loy and Mac and see if you find anything?"

"Sure enough," Slocum said.

He and the two Zig Zag riders watched as Holbrook, Jones and the others rode off in pursuit of the stolen cattle. "Slocum," said Loy, "what the hell's going on around here anyway?"

"It's just what we said before," Slocum answered. "Someone wants to get you boys shooting at each other. Either that or joining forces to wipe out the small ranchers. I don't think they give a shit which one you do first."

"God damn," Mac said. "I can't figger it."

"I don't know all the players around here well enough to figure it," Slocum said. "But it's a tough one, even if you do know them. I can tell that ole Holbrook is real aggravated by it all."

"Yeah," Loy said.

"Well, let's see if we can find anything around here," Slocum said.

But the search was fruitless. There were plenty of cattle tracks and some horse prints, but it was all a big mess. The horses could have been ridden by anyone. Loy showed Slocum approximately where both of the cowboys had fallen. Still there were no telltale signs. Finally they gave it up.

"I'm afraid there's nothing to find out here," Slocum said. "Let's see if we can catch up with those other boys."

They rode out in the wake of Holbrook and the Jones crew, following the stolen herd north on Zig Zag range.

"What the hell are they doing?" Mac said.

No one answered him. They kept on the trail. About a half hour later, Loy spoke up. "Hey," he yelled. Slocum and Mac rode over to meet him. They found him pointing at the ground. "Whoever it was," he said, "tried to cover their trail, but looky here. They turned and headed back for the Circle X."

"By God," said Slocum, "you're right. Let's go."

They rode hard after the trail. They weren't long onto the Circle X range before they met up with Jones and Holbrook riding ahead of the other hands, who were driving a herd of cattle. They sat and waited till the old man and the sheriff rode up beside them.

"You're right," Jones said. "That's the stole herd."

"Where'd you find them?" Slocum asked.

"They was put up in a blind canyon back yonder," said Jones, indicating with a thumb over his shoulder. "I had the damn thing blocked off with some barbed wire. Never used it. They cut the fence and drove them cows in there, and then they mended the fence again. We had a time finding them. The rustlers, if they can be called that, tried to cover their tracks, and they done a pretty good job of it. It was Cy here that followed them into the canyon."

"And I bet that whoever it was shot those two Zig Zag boys when they drove the herd over that way," Slocum said.

"Those poor boys just happened onto something they wasn't supposed to see," Jones said.

"That's sure what it looks like," Holbrook said. "X., has your boys here got control of things?"

"I think so. How come?"

"I'd like for you to ride over with me to see Sim."

"All right."

"Sheriff," said Loy, "if it's all right with you, me and Mac will hang around out here for a spell."

"Sure. We'll see you boys later."

Holbrook, Jones and Slocum rode toward Yates's house, while Jones's cowboys drove the newly found herd back toward home and Loy and Mac continued prowling the area. They rode across the range of the Zig Zag till they arrived at the ranch house. Sim Yates heard them coming and stepped out onto the porch. When he saw who it was, he waved. "Come on into the house," he said. The riders dismounted by the porch and went on in. Yates indicated chairs, and they all sat down.

"Can I fetch you a drink?" Yates said.

"It's a little early for me yet," Holbrook said, "but thanks."

"Coffee?"

"I'll have a cup," Holbrook said, and the others all agreed with him. Josie appeared in time to go for the pot and cups, and soon she had everyone served. "Good coffee," said Holbrook, trying hard not to give Josie any suggestive looks. Slocum noticed the effort, but he doubted that anyone else did.

"Well," said Yates, "what do we owe this visit to?"

"About a hundred head of my cattle was run off yesterday, Sim," said Jones. "We went out looking for them this morning. Whoever done it drove them over onto your range, turned north for a ways, then drove them back onto my place and tried to hide them in that damn blind canyon back up in there. You know the one."

"Yeah," said Yates. "I know it. But why would anyone steal your cows and then hide them right back on your place?"

"I don't use that canyon," Jones said. "Most everyone knows that."

"Well, yeah. I know that," said Yates.

"They tried to cover their tracks," said Slocum. "Likely they figured that no one would look in there for them."

"You mean they wanted it to look like the cattle was brought over here. They wanted you to think that I took them?"

"Maybe," said Holbrook.

"It looks like the same men that stole the cattle shot your boys," said Slocum.

"So it's like you said. It's someone else trying to start some trouble."

"Yeah," said Holbrook.

"Wait a minute," said Jones. "Why couldn't it have been some of the squatters?"

"You mean the small ranchers?" said Holbrook.

"Call them what you like," said Jones. "Why couldn't it have been some of them?"

"We had a meeting with them last night," said Holbrook. "They were all there, and I don't think that anyone had the time to do all of this and then make it to the meeting."

"Damn," said Jones. "So we're right back where we started."

"No," said Slocum. "I think we're ahead of that. You two were ready to start shooting at each other in the beginning."

Both old men looked at the floor, and Holbrook stood up. "Both of you," he said, "double up your guards. Keep someone out all the time, and tell your boys to watch out. There's someone out there who will try to kill them. They'd best be ready to shoot first or shoot faster or run like hell."

"I'd suggest that you two can put your forces together," Slocum said. "You'd have a better chance that way."

"Yeah," said Yates. "What do you say, X.?"

"I'll go along," said Jones.

"Well," said Holbrook, "me and Slocum's going to head back to town. We'll leave you two to work things out."

"Okay, Cy," said Yates, and Slocum and the sheriff walked out the door. They mounted up without saying anything more, and then they rode out to the road and turned toward town.

"I don't feel good about this, Slocum," said Holbrook.

"There ain't nothing to feel good about," Slocum said. "Rustling and killing."

"I mean, we ain't doing a damn thing other than telling everyone involved to watch their ass. We oughta be doing more than that."

"Figure out what it is we oughta be doing," said Slocum, "and we'll do it."

"Shit. You're a big help."

Slocum shrugged, and they rode on in silence for a while. Slocum pulled a cigar out of his pocket. Then he fetched out a match and struck it on his britches. Soon he was puffing away and thinking. Now and then Holbrook looked over at him with something akin to disgust on his face.

"Can you check into any recent land sales in these parts?" Slocum said.

"Land sales?"

"Yeah."

"What the hell for?"

"Oh, nothing maybe. It's just a hunch."

"What are you thinking about, Slocum?"

"Someone's wanting to get rid of ranchers around here. Right?"

"Right."

"How come?"

"Well, hell, I don't know."

"I can't think of anything except maybe he wants the land."

They rode another couple of miles without talking. Slocum continued puffing at his cigar.

"I can do that, Slocum," Holbrook said. "I'll do it as soon as we get back to town."

"Well," said Slocum, "if you can, do it without attracting no attention to what you're doing. We don't want to alert no one."

10

"Looks like Maudie's still open, Slocum. Want to grab a bite?" Holbrook said as they rode into town.

"Sure," Slocum said. "Why not?"

They took their horses to the stable first and saw that they were well put up for the night, and then they walked the distance down the street to Maudie's. There were only a couple of people left in the place, and Maudie was already cleaning up to finish the day.

"Are we too late, Maudie?" Holbrook asked.

"That depends on what you want," she said.

"What have you got that won't be no trouble?"

"Coffee's still good," Maudie said. "I've got some cold roast beef I can wrap in a piece of bread, and I got some apple pie."

"That sounds good to me," said Slocum. "All of it."

"Yeah, me too," Holbrook said. They sat down while Maudie brought out the food and coffee and put it on the table. She went back to work, and they went to work on the food. In another couple of minutes the other two people finished up, paid and left. Maudie brought more coffee over to Slocum and Holbrook.

"This is it," she said, "unless you want me to make some more."

"No," said Holbrook. "That'll be enough. It's a bit late for coffee anyhow. I think I could use a drink right about now. I think we'll let you alone and go on over to the Hogback just as soon as we finish up here."

"I got some whiskey right here," Maudie said. "I could break it out for a couple of good friends after hours."

"Well, now," said Holbrook. "That's right neighborly."

He looked at Slocum, and Slocum said, "That sounds real nice to me."

Maudie went to her front door and locked it. Then she went to the back room and returned a moment later with a bottle and three glasses. She put them on the table and pulled out a chair.

"All right if I join you?" she asked.

"I wouldn't have it no other way," said Slocum.

"Sure," said Holbrook. "Please do."

Maudie sat down and poured out three drinks. "I can use one of these right about now myself," she said. "It's been one of those days. You know?"

"Rough one, huh?" said Slocum.

"I can't complain. When I'm busy, I'm making money. There's nothing worse on the bank account than a slow and easy day."

"Hell, Maudie," said Holbrook, "you ought to be getting rich then, busy as you are."

"I wouldn't exactly say getting rich," she said, "but I guess I'm doing all right. I pay my bills on time."

"That's a lot," Holbrook said.

"You stock good whiskey," said Slocum.

"Only the best," she said.

They made some more small talk, and Maudie started to pour another round. Yawning, Holbrook held out his hand to stop her. "I think I'd best turn in," he said. "I thank you though." He took out some money and put it on the table. "Will that cover it all?"

"Sure will."

Holbrook stood up. "You coming, Slocum?" he asked.

"I think I'll have one more," Slocum said. He looked at Maudie. "That is, if you are."

"Yeah," she said. "Let's have another."

She got up to let Holbrook out the front door and locked it again behind him after he left. Slocum refilled the glasses while she was up. Maudie turned to go back to the table, but on her way, she turned the oil lamps down low. She sat down and picked up her glass. "Thanks," she said.

Slocum lifted his glass. "Here's to you, lady," he said.

She smiled, lifted her glass and touched it to his. They both drank.

"You know, cowboy," she said, "I kinda like you."

"You're a pretty nice lady yourself," he said.

She leaned toward him, and he met her halfway. Their lips came together. It was a gentle kiss at first. But it lingered and it grew more passionate. At last they broke apart. Maudie heaved a sigh.

"It's been a long time, cowboy," she said. "And I'm only good for a one-night stand."

"That's all right with me," said Slocum.

"Come with me," she said, and she stood up and started walking toward the back room. Slocum followed her. The back room was unlit except for some of the dim light coming in from the main room, where the light was already turned down low. Slocum saw a bed against the far wall. Maudie walked over there, stopped and turned to face him. She stepped out of her shoes and started to slip her full skirt down to the floor. Slocum pulled his own shirt off over his head. In another moment, they were both naked. Maudie crawled into the bed and looked up at Slocum. He went in beside her, and their arms went around one another as their lips met for another kiss. In another moment, Slocum was on top of her, his cock driven in as far as it could go, humping like crazy.

Holbrook was up early. He had slept in the jail again. He got himself ready for the day and walked over to Maudie's, only to find the door locked. He pulled the watch out of his pocket and checked the time. Maudie was running late. He started to turn and walk away, but just then Maudie appeared and unlocked the door. She opened it to let Holbrook in.

"Good morning, Cy," she said. "Sorry I'm late."

"That's all right," Holbrook said. "I just got here."

Holbrook made his way to a table as Maudie hustled back behind the counter. "I'll get the coffee going," she said. "Have it ready in a minute."

"Okay, Maudie."

Just then, Slocum came walking out of the back room adjusting the bandanna around his neck. He looked up, surprised to see Holbrook there. Holbrook was astonished. Slocum paused to compose himself. Then he walked on over to the table and sat down with the sheriff.

"I, uh, I was just—"

"Yeah," said Holbrook. "I see."

"Now, Cy—"

"I ain't said a word. Have I?"

"See that you don't."

In another few minutes, Maudie brought them coffee. They ordered their breakfasts, and she went to work on that. The two men were awkwardly silent. Maudie noticed from behind the counter. "Ain't no sense in you boys being embarrassed," she said. "I'm not."

Slocum lifted his cup for a slurp of coffee.

"What do you reckon we ought a be doing today?" said Holbrook.

"You got to check on land purchases," Slocum said.

"Oh, yeah," said Holbrook. "That's right. I was going to do that yesterday, but we come back in too late for it."

"What are you checking on?" said Maudie from behind the counter.

"Any recent land purchases," said Holbrook.

"Hell," she said, "I bought the old Brooks place a couple a months ago. Is that what you mean?"

"Well, yeah," said the sheriff. "How'd you come to do that?"

"A gal's got to look out for the future," she said. "I'll probably hang on to it for a while and then sell it for a profit."

"That makes sense," said Slocum.

"How come you're checking on it?" she asked.

Slocum and Holbrook exchanged glances. "Nothing important," Slocum said. Just then a couple more customers came in. The conversation ended. Maudie brought their breakfasts and went to see about the new customers. Slocum and Holbrook finished their meals, Holbrook paid, and they left. Out on the sidewalk, they stood side by side for a moment.

"Well, there's part of the answer," Holbrook said.

"Maudie bought a place," said Slocum. "What kind of place is it?"

"The Brooks place?" said Holbrook. "Brooks was one of the small ranchers. He gave it up a few months ago and pulled out. I sure didn't know that Maudie bought the place."

"Well, see if anyone else has been buying up land," Slocum said. "Who knows? We might be just farting in the wind."

"Yeah. Why don't you wait for me over in the office. This shouldn't take long."

"Sure thing," said Slocum. He walked on over to the sheriff's office and went in. He stoked up the stove and built a pot of coffee. Then he sat down and lit a cigar to wait for the coffee to boil. In a few minutes, Holbrook came in.

"Find out anything?" said Slocum.

"Burly Baker has bought a couple of small places in the last few months," said Holbrook. "Maudie bought the Brooks place, like she said. That's it."

"Baker, huh? That damn lawyer?"

"That's right."

"You say he's bought a couple of places?"

"Yeah."

"Folded small spreads?"

"Yeah."

"Maybe we had ought to kinda keep an eye on Mr. Baker," said Slocum.

"Kinda watch where he goes, who he meets up with? Like that?"

"Um hum. It could be interesting." He got up and poured some coffee in a cup and looked at it. He tasted it. "That's done," he said. "You want a cup?"

"Sure," said Holbrook. Slocum poured him some and handed him the cup.

"If you ain't got something else for me to do today," Slocum said, "I think I'll ride out to that Zig Zag and Circle X range where all the trouble has been going on and just kinda hang around, hide and watch, you know."

"That'd be all right, Slocum," said Holbrook. "Not a bad idea. I'll stick around here and try to watch ole Baker some."

• • •

Slocum rode out to the spot on the knoll where the shooter had hidden to ambush Joe Bob. It was the only place he knew of where he could hide and still have a good view of the range. He tied his Appaloosa to the bushes at the far side of the trees and made his way through to the other side, just as the shooter had done. He had a good view of the valley. He could see a small herd of Zig Zag cattle grazing off in the distance. At least, he assumed they were Zig Zag cattle. They were on the Zig Zag side. In another few minutes two Zig Zag riders rode by— checking on the cattle, he guessed—or maybe just keeping their eye out for any possible trouble. It was what he and Holbrook had told them to do. He kept watching. Two Circle X riders came in from the other side. They made straight for the Zig Zag hands. Slocum straightened himself up, ready for trouble.

He watched as the four riders came together. They stopped and sat on their horses talking for a spell. Then the Circle X boys turned and rode back toward their own range. Nothing happened. Maybe they were just being friendly. Cooperating in their watch. That would be good. He lit a cigar and smoked it, and nothing more happened except that a bull mounted a cow and humped her real good. After a spell, Slocum went back and got on his horse. He rode over to X. Jones's ranch house and chatted with Jones for a bit. Nothing had happened. Slocum left and rode over to the main house on the Zig Zag. Yates came out on the porch.

"Come on in, Slocum," he said.

"No, thanks, Mr. Yates. I'm just making some rounds here. Everything quiet out here?"

"So far," Yates said.

Slocum rode back to town. He tied the Appaloosa to the rail in front of the sheriff's office and went inside. No one was there. He walked out and on over to the Holbrook. Holbrook was standing at the bar. He saw Slocum coming in and called for another glass. Picking up the bottle by its neck, he turned to face Slocum.

"Come on and sit down," he said, leading the way to a table. Slocum followed, and they sat down. Holbrook poured Slocum a drink and shoved it across the table to him. "What did you find?" he asked.

Slocum shook his head. "Everything's quiet so far," he said.

"Same here. Oh, I seen a couple of Baker's customers go into his office, local businessmen. Nothing suspicious though. Slocum, we got to come up with something and that real soon."

"I don't know what we can do except to catch them at something," Slocum said. "We can do all the figuring in the world, but when you get right down to it, it's just guesswork. That's all."

"Well, something's got to give."

Slocum looked around the big room. There were quite a few men in the place. "You know everyone in here?" he asked.

Holbrook looked around. "There's a few I don't know," he said.

"You think it might be time to start checking on them all? You know, asking them who they are and what's their business, like that?"

"That's pretty heavy-handed, Slocum," Holbrook said, "but, hell, I don't know. It might come to that."

"Well, you don't have to go up to them and say what the hell are you doing in my damn town. You could quiz them up in a little bit softer way than that."

Just then Charlie Roberts burst through the batwing doors. He stopped and looked around frantically. Then he spotted Holbrook and Slocum and hurried over to their table.

"Charlie," said Holbrook, "what's wrong with you?"

"I been fighting a fire," said Roberts. "That's what."

His clothes were blackened, as were his face and hands.

"Where at?" said Holbrook.

"Bill Jackson's place," Roberts said. "It's burned to the ground. His barn and his house. It's all lost."

"That's damn bad luck," Holbrook said.

"It wasn't bad luck," said Roberts. "It was set."

"You sure of that?"

"Damn right. We could see where it was set. It was deliberate all right."

"Was anyone hurt?"

"No. Thank God for that, but Bill's damn near ruined. A bunch of us told him we'll help him rebuild. I guess he's thinking about it, but he's also thinking about clearing out. Giving up."

Slocum thought that their antagonist was getting clever. He had them watching the two big ranches, and then he struck at one of the smaller ones. "Did anyone see anyone messing around out there who shouldn'ta been there?" he asked.

"Bill saw someone riding away," said Roberts, "but the fire was going by that time. He didn't get a good look. He didn't have time. Had to fight the fire."

"God damn it," said Holbrook. "God damn it to hell."

11

Slocum and Holbrook rode back out to Bill Jackson's spread with Charlie Roberts, and they found just what Roberts had said. The place was a total loss. The corral had been built up against one side of the barn. When the barn had burned, the corral had collapsed, and the horses that Jackson had kept in there had all run off. The house and barn were nothing but a pile of rubble, a charred wreck. Jackson and some of the other small ranchers were rummaging through the mess, but they were finding very little to salvage. As the three riders approached, Jackson tossed aside what he held in his hands and looked up at the sheriff.

"You're a little late, Cyrus," he said.

"I'm sorry, Bill," said Holbrook. "Charlie said you seen someone."

"Not very good," said Jackson.

"Can you remember anything about the man?" asked Slocum.

"He was riding away from here hell-for-leather," Jackson said, "on a dark horse. That's all I know. I looked at him, and I looked at the fire, and I run to try to put the fire out. Damn fool. I just as well have chased the bastard for all the good I done here."

Holbrook dismounted and let the reins drag on the ground. "Where did it start?" he asked.

"You can't tell too much now," Jackson said, "but when I first seen it, there were four brush piles up against the walls.

Right over here, and there, and there, and there." He pointed as he spoke.

"No question that it was set deliberate?" Slocum said.

"No damn question at all," said Jackson.

"What are you going to do now, Bill?" Holbrook asked him.

"Hell, I don't know. I ain't decided yet. I feel like getting out, but I— Well, I just ain't decided. That's all."

"Charlie told me that him and some others has promised to help you rebuild," Holbrook said. "That's good neighbors. You ought to think about that."

"I'm thinking about it all right," Jackson said, "but hell, Cy, I lost everything in that fire. If I get another house, I won't have nothing to put in it. And what if the bastard just comes around and does it again?"

"I'd say you've got more here than anywhere else," Slocum said. "You got your land and some cattle scattered over it."

"I could sell it all and have something to start over with— somewhere else."

"Yeah," said Holbrook. "You could."

"Jackson," said Slocum, "that fella you saw ride outta here— which way was he going?"

"He was headed toward town," Jackson said. Slocum looked off in the direction Jackson had indicated he saw the man ride. He turned his Appaloosa and headed that direction. He rode slowly, milling around till he found some tracks. He was pretty sure they belonged to the arsonist. They indicated that the rider was in a hurry to get somewhere. Slowly, watching carefully, Slocum followed the trail. It led eventually to the road and on toward town. He kept going.

In a few minutes, Holbrook came riding up behind Slocum. "What's your damn hurry?" he shouted.

"I want to follow this trail while it's sort of fresh," said Slocum.

"You got the man?"

"I got his trail. I'm pretty sure."

"He's headed for town," Holbrook said. "Let's go."

They followed the tracks almost into Guadalupe, but when they found themselves on the edge of town, there were so many tracks that the set they were following was obscured.

"Damn it," said Holbrook. "We lost him."

"Yeah. There was nothing distinctive about those tracks either," Slocum said. "He's in town somewhere though. Let's check out the Hogback."

"Okay."

They rode to the saloon and tied their horses in front. Walking in, they looked the place over. There were several strangers in the place. Slocum and Holbrook bellied up to the bar and ordered a couple of drinks. Slocum picked up his glass and turned his back to the bar, leaning on it with his elbows. He studied the room full of cowboys and range bums. He noticed one man who seemed to be particularly nervous. He was seated at a table alone. The man finished his drink and got up to leave. To do so, he had to pass right by Slocum and Holbrook. As he was about to pass them by, Slocum reached out an arm to block his path.

"Hold up there a minute, partner," he said.

The man stopped and looked at Slocum. "What do you want?" he said.

Holbrook turned around then. "What's your name, mister?" he said.

The man looked at the star on Holbrook's vest. "I ain't done nothing, Sheriff," he said. "You got no call to go quizzing me up like that. I'm just on my way outta here."

"What's your name?"

"Harrington," the man said. "Abel Harrington. Okay?"

"You don't live around here, do you?" Holbrook asked.

"I'm living around here now," Harrington said.

"Where?"

"Just outside of town."

"Where might that be?"

"Look," Harrington said. "I don't have to—"

"Where?" asked Holbrook.

"Me and my partner, we got us a camp out by the creek. Out south."

"How'd you come to be camping outside of Guadalupe?" said Slocum.

"We're just traveling. Had to stop and rest a spell. Anything wrong with that?"

"You said that you lived here now," Holbrook said.

"Well," said Harrington with a nervous laugh, "I ain't dead."

"You just come into town for a drink, did you?" asked the sheriff.

"Yeah. That's right."

"You just ride straight in from your camp?" Slocum asked.

"That's right."

"You sure you didn't come from the opposite direction?"

"Sure I'm sure. What are you getting at?"

"We just had a little trouble out at one of the ranches," said Slocum.

"Oh, yeah?"

"Yeah," said Holbrook. "One of the small ranches was—"

Slocum elbowed Holbrook to shut him up. "Someone was out there deliberately causing trouble. We followed his trail back here."

"Well, it wasn't me. I don't know what you're talking about."

"Course, he had plenty of time, Cy," said Slocum. "He could be telling the truth. I mean, about where he came from. He had time to go back to his camp, stay awhile, hell, even wash his hands and face, change his shirt maybe, and then ride back in here. He could have come in here straight from his camp."

"Yeah," Holbrook said. "You're right about that."

"Why don't we all go over to the jail to finish talking this over?" Slocum said.

"Yeah," said Holbrook. "Come on. Let's go."

"Hey. I don't have to go to the jail with you. I—"

Slocum's Colt was out in a flash, its muzzle poking Harrington's belly. "The sheriff said let's go."

Harrington turned slowly and nervously and started walking. As he did, Slocum slipped the revolver out of Harrington's holster and tucked it in his own waistband. The three men made their way down the street to the sheriff's office and went inside. Holbrook went behind the big desk and sat down. Slocum perched on the right-hand front corner of the desk. Harrington stood nervously in front of the desk, looking from Holbrook to Slocum and back again. Neither man said anything. At last, Harrington broke the silence.

"Listen," he said, "I don't know nothing about that fire."

Slocum glanced at Holbrook.

"How'd you know we were talking about a fire?" Holbrook said.

"Huh? Well, that's what you said. Ain't it?"

"We never mentioned a fire," said Slocum. "We just said that there'd been some trouble."

"Well, maybe someone else said something. I heard it somewhere."

"Or maybe you started it," said Slocum.

"No. I never. Damn it, I never started no fire. Believe me. Look. Give me back my gun and let me get outta here. My partner'll be looking for me here pretty soon."

"What's your partner's name?" said Slocum.

"His name?"

"I think you heard me."

"His name is Tor Stark. We're cowhands. Outta work. We're just kinda looking the country over. You know? Let me go, and we'll be on our way. We'll pull out today."

Holbrook opened a desk drawer and took out his stack of wanted posters. He began flipping through them casually. "Cowhands, you say?"

"Yeah. That's right."

"Where'd you work last?"

"What?"

"Where the hell was your last damn job?" said Slocum.

"Uh, a place called the Three Corners up in Colorado."

"How long were you there?" Holbrook said.

"Oh, a few months, I guess."

"Where else?"

"Uh, the Granite. Up in Wyoming."

"You and Stark both work these places, did you?" said Holbrook.

"Yeah. Yeah. Both of us."

"You quit or get fired?"

"Well, we, uh, just decided it was time to move on. That's all."

"Tired of working?"

"No. It was just time to move on. Like I said."

"I think you got fired," Holbrook said. "You know, I can

check up on your story. I can send a wire. We ain't totally in the middle of nowhere out here."

"All right. So we got fired. So what?"

"Now maybe you'll tell us what you're really doing here in Guadalupe," said Slocum.

"I already told you," Harrington said. "We're just passing through. That's all. We just decided to stop here and rest up a few days. It was a mistake. We'll ride on now, and we won't never stop here again."

Holbrook hesitated over a dodger. He put it on the bottom of the stack and continued shuffling.

"You didn't start that fire?" he said.

"No."

"Give him back his gun, Slocum."

Slocum gave Holbrook a curious look, but he pulled out the gun and handed it back to Harrington. Harrington took it and shoved it in his holster. He looked at the sheriff.

"Go on," Holbrook said.

"You mean, I can go?"

"That's what I said. Your partner will be looking for you."

Harrington turned and hurried out of the office, slamming the door behind him. Slocum turned to stare hard at Holbrook, who was still shuffling posters.

"You make a pretty good lawman, Slocum," Holbrook said.

"I've had plenty of practice," said Slocum. "On the other side. Now, what the hell did you let him go for? He slipped up. He knew it was a fire we were investigating, and he didn't hear someone say something about it in the damn saloon."

Holbrook tossed a dodger across the desk. Then he shuffled through his stack to find the one he had slipped to the bottom earlier. He tossed it over as well. Slocum looked at them. The first one said, "Wanted, Tor Stark," and the second was the same for Abel Harrington. The reward was small. They were petty thieves, although they were suspected of a few bigger things.

"You could've locked him up," Slocum said.

"I'da had to send him back to Nevada," said Holbrook. "I thought that maybe we'd get farther watching him and his partner."

"What if they just ride on out of here like he said?"

"Then he's not our man," said Holbrook. "Or if he is, our troubles are over."

"You want me to ride out and spy on his camp?" Slocum asked.

"No," said Holbrook. "Let's both ride out there and locate it, but let's not spy. Let's be open about it. Come on."

They walked back to where they had left their horses tied in front of the saloon, mounted up and rode south. It didn't take them long to find the camp. As they rode in, the two men stood up, ready for anything. Slocum and Holbrook stayed on their horses.

"Right where he said," said Holbrook. He looked at Stark. "Are you Tor Stark?"

"That's me," Stark said. "What do you want here?"

"Nothing much," said Holbrook. "We were just talking to your partner there back in town. He told us you were living here. I like to know where folks are living around these parts. I'm Cyrus Holbrook, sheriff. This is my partner, Slocum."

"John Slocum?" Stark said.

"That's right," said Slocum.

"I've heard of you."

"That's interesting," said Slocum. "I never heard of you. Till today."

"I didn't know you were a lawman."

"A man does a lot of things in this life."

"Why don't you get down? Have a cup of coffee with us?"

"No, thanks," said Holbrook. "We came out to see where you was living. We seen it. We'll be going back to town."

"You mean that's it?"

"That's it."

Holbrook turned his horse to ride out. Slocum sat watching the two men in the camp until Holbrook was a distance away. Then he turned his Appaloosa to follow. The two outlaws stood in silence and watched them go for a while. Then Stark said, "We might have to kill them two."

"You think so?"

"It's sure enough beginning to look that a way. I'll have a talk with the boss about it first chance I get."

"Tonight?"

"Maybe tonight."

12

Things were tense in the area around Guadalupe, with everyone on the lookout for trouble and not knowing where it might be coming from or when. Charlie Roberts and the other small ranchers were still not quite convinced by Slocum and Holbrook's theory. They might be right, the ranchers thought, but then again, it could be Jones or Yates or the two of them in cahoots. Jones and Yates, on the other hand, were every bit as confused as Roberts and his bunch. They were still suspicious of the small ranchers. But they did not quite trust each other. And then again, if Slocum and Holbrook were right, it could be someone else entirely. Everyone was on edge. Holbrook was afraid that if he and Slocum did not come up with the solution, and that very soon, all hell would break loose. One day Slocum would ride around the area of the small ranches keeping his eyes open for any sign of trouble while Holbrook rode the range of the two big spreads. The next day they would switch. But even so, they both knew that they could not watch every place, every minute, that something could happen somewhere at any time.

Slocum could not decide whether he just wanted to ride away from this damn place and let whatever was going to happen go on and happen, or if he really wanted to stick around and see it through. He was pissed off at Holbrook most of the time for having conscripted him into the job. And he was not even getting any pay for it. He had ridden into Guadalupe with what he thought was plenty of cash in his jeans, but it wasn't going to last forever. Well, he could keep making Holbrook pay for his meals and his whiskey, but so far, he was having to come up with the cash for his room himself. He could go out and make himself a camp somewhere if it came down to that, but he liked having a nice bed when it was available. Maybe if worse came to worst he could start sleeping in the jail. And then there was Maudie. She had said that all she was interested in was a one-night stand, but she might be interested in another one, or several more. He would have to be careful about that though. Several such nights could lead to complications, and he did not need that in his life.

He had breakfast with Holbrook, and then they saddled up their horses. Holbrook rode toward the two big ranches, and Slocum headed out for Roberts's spread. As he rode along the lonesome road, he thought that this job had turned out to be a boring son of a bitch. Then a rifle shot sounded in the stillness of the morning. It was too close for comfort, and Slocum took a dive. The Appaloosa whinnied and trotted over to the side of the road. Again, everything was still. Slocum lay on his side playing possum, his right hand on the butt of his Colt, his head turned in the direction the shot had come from. He lay still and waited.

At last, he heard a sound, and he opened his eyes to look toward it. He saw the figure of a man coming down from the high rocks on the side of the road just up ahead. He was moving slowly and carefully as he made the descent. When he reached the bottom, he hesitated, looking in Slocum's direction. Holding his rifle ready, he started toward Slocum. Slocum sure did want the man alive, but he knew that he was not going to have time to be so particular. It was kill or be killed. He would have to act fast. The man was getting close now.

Slocum suddenly rolled quickly to his right, and the man fired a shot from his rifle that kicked dirt and rocks up all around. As the man was cranking another shell into the chamber, Slocum raised his Colt and snapped off a shot that tore into the man's chest. Slocum knew as soon as it hit the mark that it was a death shot, and he swore out loud. The man staggered and fell. He lay still. Slocum stood up and walked over to the body.

He toed it over to make sure that it was dead. There was no question about it. And the man was Abel Harrington.

"Son of a bitch," Slocum muttered.

He was not surprised that it was Harrington, but he was disgusted at himself for having killed the man. He would really have liked to question him some more. He could have made Harrington talk. He was sure of that. He wished that Holbrook had left him alone in the office with Harrington that first time. He'd have gotten the information out of the man. Damn it. But that was all over and done, and there was no use worrying about it now. He put such thoughts out of his mind and went on a search for Harrington's horse.

Out on the road to the Circle X and the Zig Zag, Tor Stark lay in wait. He was crouched behind a tree in a small grove beside the road. The space in between the trees was brush-covered. He held a Henry rifle, a bullet already chambered. He had gone to see the boss, just as he had told his partner he would, and the boss had told him to go ahead. Kill the two troublesome lawmen. Get them both at the same time. Their recent habits were well known. It shouldn't be difficult. Once Holbrook and Slocum were out of the way, the rest would be easy. It would be no trouble at all to get the various parties all shooting at one another, and the rest would all be downhill.

Stark heard the sounds of a rider coming along the road, and he stiffened, raising his rifle to his shoulder. His heart beat faster in anticipation of a killing. He got almost a sexual pleasure out of killing. Sweat broke out on his forehead as he readied himself for the shot. Then Sheriff Holbrook came into view. Stark waited. He wanted to make sure. Then he fired, and he saw the splotch of blood appear on the sheriff's chest. He saw the sheriff jerk in the saddle and try to remain sitting upright as his horse ran ahead, and he watched as the lawman finally slid off the saddle and fell to one side and the horse raced on. Stark stood up, an evil smile playing across his face. He rubbed his crotch as he started walking out of the grove and toward the body lying in the road. But he heard some unexpected riders coming, and in a panic, he turned and ran back to the trees. He kept going until he came out on the back side of the grove, where his horse waited patiently, and he quickly mounted up and rode fast across country. No one had seen him. He would make his way to town and meet Harrington. They would have a drink of celebration, and then he would go to the boss for their pay. He hurried along his way.

Loy and Mac from the Zig Zag were riding along the road when they heard the shot fired. They looked at each other.

"It might just be someone shooting a rabbit," Mac said.

"Maybe," said Loy, "but let's ride ahead real careful anyhow."

They moved along the road slowly, guns ready, watching the sides for any sign of trouble. Mac was the first one to see the riderless horse in the path ahead. "Look," he said. They moved even more cautiously. In another couple of minutes, they saw the body lying on the ground.

"Keep watching," said Loy, as he hurried his horse ahead. He stopped beside the figure of the sheriff and dismounted, calling out to Mac as he did. "It's Cy Holbrook." He knelt beside the body to examine it. "He's hit bad," he called out, "but he's still alive."

"I'll catch his horse," Mac said. "We better get him to town."

"It's closer to the ranch," Loy said. "I'll take him. You ride on into town for the doc."

Mac helped Loy load Holbrook onto his horse; then he turned his own horse back toward town and spurred it, taking off at a leap. Loy moved more slowly toward the main gate of the Zig Zag.

As Slocum slung Harrington's body over the saddle of his horse, he wondered where Stark might be. He kept his eyes open. The man could be anywhere around. Harrington had missed. Stark might be luckier. Slocum mounted his Appaloosa and, taking the reins of Harrington's horse in his left hand, started back toward town. He would drop the carcass off at Riley's undertaking establishment and then head out on the road after Holbrook. He did not think that he needed to pursue his usual rounds out around Roberts's place. Holbrook would want to know about Harrington.

•   •   •

When Slocum rode into Guadalupe and pulled up in front of Riley's, he could see that something was going on down the street, approximately in front of the sheriff's office. He was curious, but he had a body to get rid of. Through his front window, Riley had seen Slocum stop and had seen the extra horse with the corpse slung across the saddle. He came walking out on the sidewalk with a long expression on his face.

"Ah," he said, "how may I be of assistance?"

"Just plant the son of a bitch," said Slocum, "and send the bill to the sheriff's office."

Riley opened his mouth to say more, but Slocum headed on down the street. He soon reached the crowd that was gathered there, and he dismounted. "What the hell's going on?" he asked. A businessman in the front of the small gathering turned to face Slocum.

"A cowhand from the Zig Zag just rode into town to fetch the doc," he said. "They just now lit out again. Going out to the Zig Zag. The sheriff's been shot."

Slocum jumped back on his horse and took off like a shot for the Zig Zag. The businessman wasn't through talking. He shouted after Slocum. "Looks like you're in charge now."

If Slocum heard that last statement, he paid it no mind. He rode as fast as he could toward the Zig Zag. If they took the doc out there, then Holbrook wasn't killed. That was something. But he was shot. How bad? Slocum wondered.

Just as Slocum headed fast toward the Zig Zag, Tor Stark stepped back out onto the street. He saw Slocum go, and he breathed a sigh of relief. He had some fresh money in his pocket from the shooting of the sheriff. But seeing Slocum made him wonder about his partner. As he headed for his horse, he glanced down the street in the other direction, and he saw Riley out in front of his place with a horse and a body. He recognized the horse. It was Harrington's. That had to be Harrington draped across its back. It had to be, but Stark wanted to make sure. He rode casually down that direction.

When he reached Riley's place, Riley had gone back inside for a gurney. Stark rode over close to the horse and looked at the body. It was Harrington all right. God damn it, he thought. He debated what to do next. He had money in his pockets. It would be a good time to leave. Just get the hell out while the getting was good. But there was more money to be made, and although he had not been all that fond of Harrington, the stupid fool, Harrington had been his partner, and the man who had killed him was still running loose. He knew that the boss would pay him well for gunning Slocum, and he himself would get one hell of a thrill over that particular killing. He would have to move his camp and stay hidden until he got his chance.

He had to think fast. He had a little time. Slocum had just ridden away lickety-split toward the Zig Zag, obviously to check on Holbrook. Stark had to go see the boss again and get clear on the deal to do away with Slocum. Then he had to get out to his camp and pack it up. He would have to locate a new site for his camp. Then he would have to make plans for getting Slocum. He was disappointed that he had not killed Holbrook. He would have, had those riders from the Zig Zag not come along when they did. But at least he had put the sheriff out of commission for a while. And who knew? Holbrook might die anyhow. He wasted no time in getting back to see the boss.

Slocum turned in at the main gate to the Zig Zag. He was almost to the porch, when Loy met him along the way. "He's in the house, Slocum," Loy said. "Last I checked, he was still unconscious. He was hit pretty bad. The doc's in there with him." Slocum rode on to the house, dismounted and tied his horse to the rail there in front of the porch. He took the stairs two at a time, strode across the porch to the front door, opened it and walked on in without knocking. Sim Yates was sitting in an easy chair in the front room.

"Howdy, Slocum," Yates said.

"Howdy. Is Holbrook—"

"He's back yonder in the bedroom. Doc's with him. So is Josie. Won't do you no good to go in there now. Cy's unconscious. Sit down here with me and wait. You want some coffee? A drink?"

"It's a little early in the day," Slocum said. "I'll have some coffee. Keep your seat. Just point me to it."

"No," said Yates. "I'll fetch it for you. I'm feeling pretty useless just now. Sit down."

Slocum took a chair as Yates went for the coffee. When the old man brought it back and handed it to Slocum, Slocum said, "Thanks." He took a tentative sip, and then he looked over at Yates, who was back in his easy chair. "You said you were feeling worthless. I feel like I've just been played for a chump."

"How's that?"

"They hit you all out here for a while," Slocum said, "and got us to watching out this way. Then they caught us off guard, hit one of the small ranches. Me and Holbrook was taking turns riding out in both directions, and then they hit us both at the same time. The one that hit Cy was luckier than the one that tried for me. Even so, I feel like I've been played for a chump, and Cy's in there with a bullet in him. Do you have any idea how bad he was hit?"

Yates just shook his head. "Doc says it's bad. That's all he'd say."

"Damn it," said Slocum.

"Did you get the one that tried for you?" said Yates.

"I killed the son of a bitch," said Slocum. "I didn't have no choice. It was him or me. I'd much rather have caught the bastard alive."

"Tough luck. Who was it? Do you know?"

"A hired gun who called himself Abel Harrington. He was camped outside of town with his partner. Tor Stark was his name. Me and Holbrook dropped in on their camp the other day for a visit. Kind of like to let them know we was watching them. Now it looks like that mighta been a mistake."

"You reckon it was that Stark then that shot Cy?"

"I'd bet a whole bunch of money on it," said Slocum.

"Anyone else with them?"

"Not that we know of."

"Then you think it was them two behind all this trouble?"

"I'd guess someone in town was paying them," Slocum said. "I wish I had an idea who."

"So what do you do now? Go after this Stark?"

"I don't think I'll have to," Slocum said. "I figure Stark will come after me."

The bedroom door opened, and Josie stepped out. The worry showed on her face. She saw Slocum and walked over to him. He stood up as she approached. Josie walked into his arms and put her head on his shoulder. Slocum put his arms around her. He patted her on the shoulder.

"How is he?" he asked.

She straightened up and stepped back. "He's hurt bad. Doc's done all he can for now. He said it's a good thing that Loy brought him here instead of heading for town. He wouldn't have made it."

"Is he going to make it now?"

She shook her head. "We just don't know yet," she said. "Wait and see."

The bedroom door opened again. This time, Doc poked his head out. "Josie?" he said. "He's awake now. He wants to see you."

Josie hurried to the door and stepped inside. Slocum stood up and paced the floor. In a few minutes, Josie looked out. "John," she said. "Would you come in?"

13

Slocum walked in and found Holbrook looking white as a sheet, with his eyes about halfway opened and his breathing heavy. "Don't stay too long, Mr. Slocum," said the doc.

Slocum walked to the head of the bed and looked down at the wretched sheriff. "Cy," he said, "you don't need to say a damn thing. They tried to get me, but it didn't work out. I killed the son of a bitch who tried it. It was that damned Harrington, so I know who shot you. Tor Stark. I'll get him, Cy. You just relax and get well."

He started to turn and leave, but Holbrook raised one hand just a little and spoke in a harsh whisper. "Slocum. Wait."

"What is it, Cy?"

"You don't have to, Slocum," said Holbrook. "I lied to you about the conscription. You're free to go."

"This is a fine time to tell me that, you son of a bitch," Slocum said. "They tried to kill me, and you too. You know damn well I ain't going to leave now."

"Then you're acting sheriff," said Holbrook. "Doc, you're my witness to this. You're on the payroll, too, Slocum. Go get the dirty bastard."

Holbrook's eyes shut, and he seemed to have gone back to sleep. The doc checked him quickly. "He's resting," he said.

"I'll be going," said Slocum. He walked out of the room and headed for the front door. Yates sat up straight as he walked by.

"How's Cy?" he said.

"He went back to sleep," said Slocum.

"After he made Slocum acting sheriff," said Josie, who had come out of the bedroom just after Slocum. "It was a good decision."

"He didn't have a hell of a lot of choice now, did he?" Slocum said.

"I still say it was a good one."

"Yeah," said Yates. "I agree. What are you going to do now, Sheriff?"

"Don't call me that," said Slocum. "I'm going after that god damned Stark."

He opened the door, and as he was walking out, he heard Josie say, "Be careful, Slocum."

Outside, Slocum managed to locate Loy and ask where he and Mac had found Holbrook. Loy rode along with him to the spot. Slocum thanked him and sent him on back to the ranch. Then he rode slowly around studying the ground until he found the ambush spot. From there he found where the horse had been tied, and he followed the tracks back toward town. About a mile out, he lost them, due to the heavy traffic. Slocum figured that Stark had gone into town to report to his boss, whoever the hell that might be. He had likely also expected to meet up with Harrington, thinking that the two of them would celebrate their success with a drink.

Perhaps the son of a bitch had even been in town when Slocum rode in with the body. In a way, Slocum hoped that he had been. He hoped that Stark had seen Harrington lying limp across his horse's back. He hoped that Stark had also seen Mac ride out of town with the doctor in tow, so that he would know that he, too, had been unsuccessful.

Slocum went to the hotel and paid his bill. Then he went to his room and packed up his few belongings. He carried them on over to the sheriff's office and tossed them in one of the cells. That would be his home now for a while. He rummaged through the drawers in Holbrook's desk until he found some keys. He tried them out, finding that one of them was an extra key to the front door. He put that one in his pocket and returned the others to the desk drawer. Then he sat down behind the desk.

The door opened and Burly Baker came striding into the office.

"Slocum," he said. "I heard that Cy was shot."

"You heard right," said Slocum, adding in his mind, *you son of a bitch.*

"He name you acting sheriff?"

"He did."

"I'm not sure that he can do that," said Baker. "That might call for an act of the town council."

"Oh yeah? That's the first I've heard of a town council around here. Pretty active, is it?"

"Well, we haven't met for a while, but—"

"If you're uncomfortable with the title, just call me a deputy. You never complained when he made me a deputy."

"Well, he's got the authority to name deputies, but not an acting sheriff."

"Call me whatever you like," said Slocum. "It won't make any difference anyhow."

"What do you mean by that?"

"Just what I said."

"I get the feeling you don't like me, Slocum," said Baker.

"I don't know you," said Slocum, "but I don't like your profession worth a damn."

Baker pulled a chair over to the desk and sat down, looking across at Slocum. Slocum pulled out a cigar and a match and lit his stogie. A big cloud of smoke rose between him and the lawyer. Baker coughed.

"The world's got to have lawyers, Slocum," Baker said.

"It's got too damn many as far as I can tell."

"I'm the only one in town."

"That speaks well for Guadalupe. One's already too many. Tell me something, lawyer. Why would anyone want to run all these ranchers out of business?"

"I don't have a clue," Baker said.

"Then I've got no more use for you than for any other citizen of this town."

Baker stood up and glared at Slocum for a moment. "I'll be seeing you around," he said, and he turned and walked out the door. Slocum heaved a sigh and looked at the big desk in front of him. In disgust, he stood up, walked around it and headed for the door.

He spent some time walking around town looking for Stark's horse. He didn't really expect to find it, but it was something to do.

He waited until after one o'clock so the crowd would be thinned out, and then walked over to Maudie's for some lunch. She still had a few customers, but she took Slocum's order in a short while. The customers left one at a time, and soon Maudie had served Slocum's meal. He was the last one in the place, and Maudie poured herself a cup of coffee and sat down to join him.

"I hope you don't mind," she said.

"Hell, no," he said. "I'm glad for the company. Ain't you going to eat?"

"Not yet," she said. "Say, I heard some talk."

"What about?"

"Cy."

"He's been shot," Slocum said.

"Not killed?"

"No. At least, not yet."

"Have you seen him?"

"We had a few words before he went back to sleep."

"Well, what did he have to say? Did he know who shot him?"

"He told me he lied about that conscription business," Slocum said. "He said I was free to go. I told him I'd stick around."

"You didn't answer my question."

"He didn't see who shot him," said Slocum, "but it don't matter. I know who it was."

"How could you know?"

"On account of the bastard's partner tried to kill me. I got him instead."

"You know for sure the two men are partners?"

"I know it."

"Well, I sure wish you luck," Maudie said, "and I hope Cy pulls through all right."

"He's a tough son of a bitch," said Slocum. "I think he'll pull through."

"Slocum?"

He looked up at her, a question in his eyes.

"Slocum," she said, "if you want to, you can drop by here tonight. After I close up."

He finished chewing his mouthful and swallowed. "Thanks, Maudie. It's a tough offer to turn down, but I think I'll spend the night in the jail. I got my reasons. Can I take a rain check?"

"Sure," she said. "Anytime."

When he finished his meal, he saddled up his Appaloosa and rode out to the place where Harrington and Stark had been camped. He found what he had expected. The campsite had been abandoned. It had not been cleaned up however. He looked around for a few minutes before he determined that there was nothing to be learned there. Then he rode back to town.

Was it possible, he wondered, that Stark had left town? He didn't hardly think so. Then the man would have had to relocate his camp. Or could someone have been putting him up secretly? Slocum could not imagine who could be doing that. He did not really believe that the murdering Stark had just ridden out though. Obviously there was still work to be done, and he would want to bleed it for all it was worth. He might not give a shit about his dead partner, but Slocum thought that he would want to get the man who killed Harrington, if for no other reason than for pride. He was probably still around, and he would be looking for an opportunity to kill Slocum.

Slocum knew that he would have to be on his guard. Stark was not the kind to call a man out. He had already proven that he would much more likely shoot from hiding and shoot a man in the back. Slocum meant to be more careful with Stark than he had been with Harrington. He wanted Stark alive so he could question him. He wanted to find out who was behind all this. Maybe if Stark was threatened with a hanging, he would decide that he did not want to hang alone.

The day dragged by slowly, with Slocum feeling at loose ends. When evening arrived, he went to the Hogback for a drink. He had several. There was no one interesting in the place and nothing really happening. He left and walked on over to the sheriff's office. He tossed his hat on the desktop and walked into the cell where he had thrown his belongings. Sitting down on the cot, he pulled off his boots. He took off his shirt, and then he unbuckled his gunbelt. Stretching out on the cot, he put the gunbelt beside him. His mind was racing with thoughts, but eventually, he dropped off to sleep.

When the sound of the front door opening woke him up, he had no idea what time it was or how long he had slept. Slowly and quietly, he slipped the Colt out of the holster and held it ready. Then he heard his name called softly.

"Slocum?"

He shoved the Colt back in the holster and sat up.

"I'm in here," he said.

Maudie came walking around the corner. "You didn't say that you didn't want any company in here," she said.

"No. I didn't."

"Do you mind?"

"Come right in," he said. "If you don't mind being in a jail cell."

"It'll be different," she said.

He stood up as she walked in, and she reached her arms around his shoulders, pulling him to her. She parted her lips as they met his, and she probed his mouth with her tongue. Slocum's blood began to race faster through his veins, and the rod between his legs started to swell and rise. Pressing her body against his, Maudie felt it coming to life. She broke loose from his embrace long enough to get out of her clothes. Slocum finished undressing himself while she was dropping her clothes onto the jail cell floor. She sat beside him on the cot, and as he kissed her again, she lay back, Slocum moving on top of her, feeling her nakedness against his own. Her hands reached down between his legs to stroke the now swollen member there. She clutched it hard, and it bucked in her hands.

"Here," she said. "Right here."

She guided it into her waiting pussy, and it slipped easily into the juicy tunnel. Slocum pumped slowly at first, then faster. As he drove down, she responded by thrusting her hips upward to meet him. Slocum's heavy balls bounced against her ass as he pounded furiously in and out. All of a sudden, he stopped to catch his breath.

"Wait," said Maudie. "Let me turn over."

Slocum withdrew himself, and Maudie squiggled around until she was on her hands and knees on the cot. Slocum looked at the round ass that thrust itself up at him, and he aimed for the hole again and rammed himself in. "Ah," she said. "That's good. Fuck me, Slocum. Fuck me." He slapped himself against her ample ass again and again, driving his hot cock deeply inside her. "Let me have it," she said. Slocum pumped a few more times. Then he slipped himself loose. "What are you doing?" she said.

"Let me lay down," he said.

She got out of his way, and he stretched out on the cot, his cock standing straight up. "Oh," she said, and she straddled him, letting herself down on the stalk, allowing it to slip slowly into her wetness. "Ah," she said. "That's good. That's very good." She began to rock herself back and forth, sliding her sweating butt and thighs over his crotch. She moved faster and faster until she groaned out loud. "God," she said, "I'm coming."

"Come ahead," Slocum said.

She lowered herself down until her breasts were mashed against his chest, and her lips crushed themselves against his. At last, she straightened up again and started to rock again. Soon she came again, and again. She was rocking furiously yet again, when Slocum felt the pressure build in his balls. He humped against her, thrusting upward, and suddenly he burst forth, sending a gusher spurting up into her dark and cavernous hole. She fell forward against him once more, and they lay still for a moment as his juices ran down onto her thighs and his.

At last, she got up and went to look for a towel. Finding one, she wiped at her crotch. Finishing with it, she tossed it to Slocum. He caught the towel, and she began picking up her clothes and getting dressed.

"Are you leaving?" he asked her.

"Yeah," she said. "I've got to get back."

"Okay," he said. "I'm sure glad you came by."

"Me too. Maybe we'll do it again sometime."

"I hope so."

Suddenly she was gone, and Slocum sat alone and naked in the jail cell. He stood and walked over to the desk, opening a drawer. He found the bottle and a glass and poured himself a drink. He put the cork back in the bottle and the bottle back in the drawer. Then he walked back to the cell and sat on the cot. It had been a strange encounter, he thought, but then, he figured, women must get horny just the same as men. That must have been all she wanted. He guessed that was all right with him. He took a sip of whiskey and leaned back against the wall.

14

The next day, Slocum made his rounds, out to the small ranches and over to the Circle X and the Zig Zag. He found nothing out of the ordinary. While he was in the vicinity of the Zig Zag, he looked in on Cy Holbrook. He found Holbrook resting fairly well. It seemed that the sheriff would pull through after all. Slocum reported to Holbrook that he had not yet come across Stark, but he assured him that he had not given up.

"I'll find that bastard if he ain't left the country," he said.

"I know you will," said Holbrook, in a labored whisper.

"You rest easy, pard," Slocum said. "I'll do everything I can."

"Don't go crazy killing folks," said Holbrook.

"I'll try to do it all the way I think you would."

Holbrook smiled and closed his eyes. He still tired easy. Slocum slipped out of the room to let him sleep. Josie met him in the living room. "How's he look to you, Slocum?" she asked.

"Well, ma'am," he said, "it don't hardly seem right. It's been such a short time since he was shot, but he looks to me a whole lot better than what he did yesterday. I think he'll pull through all right."

Josie smiled. "I think you're right," she said. "He's a strong man."

"You know, Josie," said Slocum, "he's real stuck on you."

"Oh?"

"I might could be speaking out of turn. I been known to do

100

that. But I know ole Cy pretty good by now, and I'm afraid he ain't spoke his mind to you. Am I right?"

"Go on, Mr. Slocum," she said.

"Well, he told me that you had kind of offered him a job out here, but he said that he couldn't quit sheriffing as long as there was trouble around here. And he don't feel like he could ask a woman to marry up with him as long as he's a sheriff. You know, he couldn't ask a woman to sit at home waiting to hear if he'd been shot—or something." He paused, considering the irony of what had happened just the day before. "I guess someone just proved him right about that," he added.

"I'm not soft, Slocum," Josie said. "I can take it. If that's what's stopping Cy Holbrook, he can just try to come up with a better excuse."

"Well, maybe he'll quit that job as soon as we straighten up this mess we're in right now."

"If he's using that as an excuse," Josie said, "he'll just come up with another one. That's the way it works."

Slocum didn't like the way this conversation was going. He was thinking that he should have just minded his own business. But that was the way of it. He was always blundering into something that was none of his affair. Just look at the mess he was involved in. Hunting a killer. Trying to figure out who the son of a bitch was working for. Getting his ass shot at. Would he never learn?

"Yeah," he said. "Well, excuse me, ma'am. I'd best be getting on."

As he reached the door and was about to leave, Josie said, "Slocum. I know you were just trying to help. Thanks."

He touched the brim of hat and nodded. Then he went on out the door and mounted the Appaloosa. "Come on," he said. "Let's go." He rode out of the Zig Zag ranch faster and harder than he needed to, wondering what the hell was his hurry.

Back in town, he had his lunch at Maudie's, and then he went back over to the sheriff's office. He tried thinking about the problems he was facing, but that did no good. He was just marking time. There was nothing to be done. All he could do was wait for the other side to make some kind of a move. The idleness and frustration was getting to him. He decided to go over to the Hogback and have a drink. First he lit a cigar. Puffing all the way, he walked to the saloon.

Bellied up to the bar, he called for whiskey. Amos brought a clean glass and a bottle. He poured a drink and started to take the bottle away, but Slocum stopped him. "Leave it," he said. He put some money on the counter, and Amos took it and replaced it with some change. Slocum let the change stay on the bar as he lifted the glass for a sip. It tasted good as it burned its way down his throat and into his belly. It was so good, he decided to drink it all down in a gulp. He did so and poured himself a second drink. He figured he'd sip this one.

He glanced down toward the far end of the bar, where a man was eating hard-boiled eggs out of a bowl on the bar and nursing a large glass of beer. A couple of other men were standing nearby. Now and then one of them went for one of the eggs. Slocum looked away. Then he looked back quickly. It was Stark. The son of a bitch. The arrogant bastard. Showing himself like that right in town in the middle of the day. Just who the hell did he think he was dealing with?

Maybe the silly shit thought that with Holbrook out of commission, Slocum would no longer be on the job. Well, he had another think coming. Maybe Stark could let his partner get killed and just go on about his business. But Slocum wasn't like that. No one could ambush Slocum's partner and get away with it. He picked up his glass and his bottle and headed for the far end of the bar. He stopped there, still at the front of the bar, just where it made a sharp corner. Stark was near him, but around the corner. He was just reaching for another egg.

"I didn't expect to see you here, you sorry ass chicken snake," said Slocum.

Stark lifted the egg and held it in front of his face. Slowly he looked over at Slocum. "Why not?" he said.

"Why not?" said Slocum. "Where you come from, don't they take shooting a sheriff in the back very serious?"

"You can't pin that on me, Slocum," Stark said.

"The hell I can't. I know damn well you done it. I know it as well as you do."

"You think you know," Stark said. He took a bite out of the

egg and talked as he chewed. "But you go to trying to prove it, you'll play hell."

"Your partner tried to gun me the same way," Slocum said. "Right about the same time, too. He's dead."

"You talking about ole Abel Harrington? Hell, me and him split up. We broke camp, and he rode out on his own. I ain't got no idea where he went to."

"I bet."

"Well, it's the truth. That's all I got to say, and you can't prove no different."

"I'll tell you what, Stark," Slocum said. "It ain't my job to prove a damn thing. All I got to do is accuse you and arrest you. The rest will be up to a judge and jury."

"Bullshit," said Stark, as he reached for another egg.

Slocum reached over and grabbed Stark's wrist in a steel grip, holding the fist and egg just away from the open mouth.

"Swallow it whole, you damn snake," he said.

"I can't do that," Stark said.

Slocum drew his Colt with his free hand. He put the muzzle close to Stark's temple and thumbed back the hammer. The saloon grew quiet.

"Swallow it," said Slocum. "You're a snake."

Stark leaned forward, sucking the whole egg into his mouth. He did not swallow. He stood there, his eyes opened wide, his cheeks puffed out.

"Swallow," said Slocum.

Stark tried to swallow. He gagged. He coughed and spit out pieces of egg all over the bar and in his glass of beer. Then he started to heave and puke. He looked like he would choke to death. Slocum let go of the wrist to protect himself from the flying filth, but he stepped around behind Stark and relieved him of his revolver, tucking the weapon into his own waistband. Then he stepped back. He picked up his own glass and sipped from it calmly while Stark continued his gagging and puking.

At last, Stark was done. He leaned on the bar with both hands, gasping for breath. Finally he wiped his face on his shirt-sleeve. He stood panting for another moment. Then he glanced over at Slocum. He reached for his six-gun but found an empty holster.

"You can't do this," he said. "It ain't legal."

"You forget," Slocum said, "I ain't a regular lawman. Get going."

"Where?"

"To the jail."

Stark started walking slowly toward the batwing doors, staggering some as he went. Slocum drained his glass. Then with his free hand he picked up the bottle and followed Stark, holding his Colt aimed at the man's back all the way. As he walked out the door, he could hear the men in the bar start talking again. Out on the street, people watched in curiosity as Slocum marched Stark to the jail. When they at last reached it, Slocum made Stark walk into a cell, not the one he was using for his own bedroom. Then he shut and locked the door.

"You can't do this to me," Stark said.

"I just done it," said Slocum. "You want to write out a complaint? Or can't you write?"

"You bastard," Stark said. "You humiliated me in the saloon in front of everyone."

"Humiliated," said Slocum. "That's a pretty big word for you to be using. I'm surprised at you."

"God damn you."

"You just as well shut the hell up," said Slocum. "You ain't getting out. Not till your trial comes up."

"When will that be?"

"I got no idea. I don't even know how to set it up. I guess we'll just have to wait for poor ole Holbrook to heal up enough to take care of it himself."

"What?"

"You heard me."

"You mean to just leave me set here like this? For who knows how long?"

"That's about it."

"You can't do that!"

"You keep telling me what I can do and can't do," said Slocum, "but you're in the jail. Who you going to get to help you?"

"I want a lawyer."

"There's only one in town," said Slocum. "Maybe he'll come

around to see you, but I doubt it. In the meantime, if you want to do some talking to help pass the time, I'll listen."

"Talking about what?" said Stark.

"Who you been working for?"

"No one. Me and Harrington was just riding through. That's all. He decided to go his own way."

"Harrington tried to kill me," said Slocum, "and you shot Holbrook. I know that, and you know it. Who were you working for?"

"I told you," said Stark. "No one."

"Stay there and rot for all I care," Slocum said. "You're lucky you ain't dead. You would be if I hadn't made a promise to the sheriff."

He picked up his bottle and headed for the door.

"Where you going?" called Stark.

"You interrupted my drinking," said Slocum. "I'm going back to finish it."

"Wait. Wait a minute. God damn you."

Stark was still screaming when Slocum walked out of the office. He could hear the yelling halfway across the street. He went back into the Hogback and got a fresh glass, taking glass and bottle to a table. He sat down and poured another drink. Watching over the crowd, he sipped his whiskey.

At the bar, one cowboy shoved another. The scene was about to erupt into a fight, when a third man stepped in and said something. All three men looked in Slocum's direction. They turned back to the bar and lifted their drinks. In another minute, the biggest of the cowboys there at the bar turned and walked slowly over to where Slocum was sitting alone. He stood there politely. Slocum looked up at him.

"Something I can do for you?" he said.

"Yeah," the cowboy said. "If you don't mind. That man you took off to jail, could you tell me what he done?"

"That's the son of a bitch that shot your sheriff from ambush," Slocum said.

"He done that?"

"Yes, sir," said Slocum. "He did."

"Well, I be god damned," the cowboy said. "Well, that was

a good job, Mr. Slocum. A hell of a job. Excuse me. Thank you."

The cowboy went back to his buddies at the bar, and they huddled together to talk. Slocum figured they were talking about him and Stark. Pretty soon, everyone in the Hogback would know why Slocum had hauled Stark off. He had a couple more glasses of whiskey, but he'd already had his fill of the place. He took his bottle and left. He was walking toward the jail, but he stopped on the sidewalk and stood for a moment thinking. He didn't really relish sleeping in the cell next to Stark. The bastard would be blathering all night long. He thought about going back to the hotel, but he had checked out of there and taken all his belongings with him. At last he decided that his Appaloosa would be better company for the night than would Stark. He walked toward the stable.

In the Hogback, one man stood at the batwing doors watching Slocum go. He went back to the bar. "He's headed for the stable," he said.

"The stable?" said another.

"Then Stark's alone in the jail," said one.

"This is our best chance."

"I ain't so sure we had oughta be doing this," said one.

"Then keep out of it," said another. "No one's twisting your arm."

"Well, are we just going to talk about it here all night, or are we going to do it?"

"Let's go do it."

The big cowboy who had questioned Slocum led the way to the door. He was followed by seven more. As they went through the batwing doors, four more men got up from their tables and followed. Along the way, one cowboy stopped by his horse at the hitching rail and picked up his rope.

"Come on," someone called out. "Let's get the son of a bitch."

15

Slocum shifted some hay around on the floor of the stall where his big Appaloosa was stabled. He placed his saddle on the floor for a pillow. Taking off his hat, he hung it on a nail, and he sat down to pull off his boots. Then he unbuckled his gunbelt and stretched out on the floor with his Colt within easy reach. He settled down for a good night's rest.

Out on the street, the mob from the saloon had grown, and it was moving toward the sheriff's office. The creatures that formed the mob made no bones about their purpose. All along the way they picked up more followers. When they reached the jail, they found the door unlocked. The big man who had started the whole thing stepped in first, gun in hand. He paused and looked around. There was no one in sight other than Stark in his cell. Stark sat up quickly.

"Who are you?" he said.

"You don't care who I am," said the man. Then glancing over his shoulder, he called out, "Come on in, boys. It's all clear."

The mob burst into the office. Several rushed over to the cell. "Find the key," someone yelled. A man ran behind the big desk and jerked open drawers, rummaging until he found some keys. "Here's some," he said. He tossed them across the room to one of the men standing by the cell door. The man caught them and began trying keys in the lock.

"Hurry it up," someone said.

"What's going on?" said Stark.

"You'll find out."

"What the hell are you doing?"

The man with the keys unlocked the door and swung it wide open. Stark backed to the far wall and pressed himself against it. "Hey. Get out of here," he said. "Leave me alone. Leave me alone."

Four men were suddenly around him, grabbing at him, clutching his shirt and dragging him out of the cell. The rest of the mob pressed against him, but none of the others could get close enough to put hands on him. Someone poked him in the gut. Someone else smacked him across the head.

"Let me go," Stark said. "Let me go. I'll leave the county."

"Shut up," someone snapped.

They dragged and shoved him through the office and out the front door onto the sidewalk. He tried to stop his forward progress by planting his feet, but the men dragged him off the sidewalk into the street.

"Put me back in jail," Stark yelled. "You can't do this. This ain't legal."

"Shut up, Stark," said the big man. "You shot Cy Holbrook, and you're going to hang."

"What? No. He ain't dead. Even if I done it, he wasn't killed. You can't hang me for a botched job like that. I didn't do it."

"You done it all right. You prob'ly killed them cowhands, too. Well, you ain't going to kill no more."

"I didn't do it, I tell you."

They dragged Stark right past the stable, heading for a tall oak tree just on the edge of town, and as they passed by the stable, Slocum rolled over. He heard the noise outside. He muttered to himself and rolled over again, but the crowd noise continued. He wondered what the hell was going on out there. He sat up and pulled on his boots. Then, taking his gunbelt, he stood up, grabbed his hat and headed for the door. As he swung the big stable door open, he could see the back of the mob moving away from him. It took him a moment to figure out what was going on. He ran to catch up.

"Hey," he yelled. "Hey, hold up there."

The mob stopped moving. It turned to face Slocum. It was short of the oak tree by only a few steps. Slocum stopped. He buckled the belt around his waist. Looking up again, he saw that the mob had moved apart, revealing the four men who held Stark, right in the middle. Stark looked at Slocum. He was a chance.

"Slocum," he said. "Take me back to jail. They mean to hang me. You can't let them hang me. You're the law."

"Slocum," said the big man, "you ain't going to try to fight all of us, are you?"

"I hope it don't come to that," Slocum said. "No harm's been done. Not yet. Why don't you men just walk away from him and go on back to the Hogback. I'll take Stark back to his cell."

"We ain't going to do that, Slocum," the big man said. "He shot Cy. He most likely killed them cowboys. They was all friends of ours. If we let him go to trial, he's liable to get off. No one seen him. So why don't you just turn around and make like you never seen us?"

"I promised Cy that I'd handle things the way he would," Slocum said.

"Cy ain't here."

"Thanks to Stark."

"He's going to hang, Slocum. Right here and now."

"Slocum, you can't let them do it," Stark said.

Slocum studied the situation. At best, he could shoot two or three of the men. The rest of them would get him for sure. Then with him laying there dead in the dirt, they would go on and hang Stark just the same. That didn't make any sense to Slocum. Sure, he had made his promise to Cy Holbrook, but he had not promised to commit suicide. He wondered just what Cy would have done if he'd been here faced with this same predicament. There was no guarantee that the sheriff would have played the hero either. As far as Stark was concerned, Slocum had no feelings. He would have liked the chance to question him further, but he wasn't at all sure that it would do any good. He was a closemouthed son of a bitch. But, no, Slocum would not shed any tears over Stark's demise.

"You going to give him back to me?" Slocum asked.

"No way," said one.

"You can try to take him, Slocum," said the big man.

"I ain't going to fight you," Slocum said.

"Take him on over to the tree, boys," the big man ordered, and the four men who had Stark started moving. Stark's knees gave out then. Had the men not been holding on to him, he would have fallen to the ground. They dragged him underneath a high and large branch, and the cowboy with the rope swung the loop end high and over the branch.

"Slocum," screamed Stark. "You gotta stop this. Slocum? Slocum, stop this. You can't let this happen. Slocum."

He was sagging in the arms of the four men. No one had brought a horse. The cowboy put the loop around Stark's neck. Stark continued screaming at Slocum. The noose was pulled tight. The cowboy started to haul away at the other end of the rope, but he found the weight a little too much to handle. Stark coughed and gagged as the noose tightened around his neck.

"Someone give me a hand here," the cowboy said.

Two more men ran to the rope and grabbed hold. The three men managed to drag Stark screaming to his feet. They pulled harder and lifted him off the ground a couple of inches. Terror showed on the face of Stark. They pulled harder, and three more men ran over to take hold and pull. They had Stark then a few feet off the ground, and he was kicking and gagging. Drool ran down his chin. His eyeballs were opened so wide that it looked as if they would pop out of his head. His tongue protruded out of his mouth. He kicked hard with both feet, trying, it seemed, to climb up in the air in order to loosen the knot around his neck. He began to spin.

The men holding on to the rope moved slowly until they had wrapped it around the oak tree several times. Then they let go, and the rope took hold around the tree trunk. Stark was still spitting and gagging and kicking. Everyone in the mob stood still and silent, staring up at the fascinating and horrifying spectacle. Slocum, too, watched, wondering all the while what kept his eyes trained on the ghastly scene.

Suddenly the air was filled with a foul odor that crept through the mob slowly but surely and made them all want to gag.

"What the hell is that?" someone asked.

"He's shit his pants," said another.

"God, let's get out of here."

"He's got to be dead," said the big man.

They stood around for a moment longer, some holding their noses, others holding handkerchiefs or bandannas over their noses and mouths. At long last, the body was still. It hung there spinning slowly and smelling horribly. The big man spoke up at last. "Let's go," he said, and the entire mob turned and started walking back toward the Hogback. The big man stopped in front of Slocum.

"We just saved the county a lot of money," he said. "That's all."

"You took away a chance I had of finding out who he was working for," Slocum said.

"You gonna arrest me?"

"I don't think we could find a jury around here that would convict you. Otherwise I would."

"We done the best thing, Slocum. We just hurried justice along. That's all."

"You did a hell of a sloppy job of it," Slocum said.

The big man looked back over his shoulder at the dangling body. Then he looked back at Slocum. "He's still dead," he said, and he started walking in the footsteps of the rest of the mob. Slocum turned to look at the man's back.

"Hey," he called.

The man stopped and turned back to face Slocum.

"What?"

"You're the one responsible for all this," Slocum said. "You'd better send someone over to Riley's to tell him to clean up your mess."

"I'll do it," the man said, and he walked on.

Slocum stared after him for a while. Then he started walking toward the sheriff's office. There was a bottle in there, and he wanted a drink. He did not want to go to the Hogback with that mob in there. He had no desire to see any of them again, but especially not just now. He walked slowly, just feeling. He wasn't thinking. There was nothing to think about. He made it to the office and found the door standing wide open. He wasn't surprised. He walked in leaving it that way. Around the desk, he opened the drawer that contained the bottle. He took it out, uncorked it and tossed the cork aside. He turned the bottle up and took a long drink.

Taking the bottle with him, he walked outside to a chair that stood there on the sidewalk just outside the sheriff's office. He sat down there to drink. From where he sat, he could see the body, in silhouette, swinging slowly in the breeze, spinning still, but not so fast as before. Suddenly Slocum wanted to be out of Guadalupe. Far away. Taking the bottle with him, he walked back to the stable. He saddled his Appaloosa, mounted up and rode out of town.

He stopped a few miles outside of town and let the Appaloosa graze and drink at will. He himself sat down on the ground beneath a tree and leaned back against the trunk. He lifted the bottle and tilted it back, taking a huge swallow. He was trying to wash away the ugly memory of not so long ago, but it wasn't working worth a damn. He took another swallow. He felt light-headed and a little dizzy, but the image of the screaming wretch with the rope around his neck was as clear as ever in his mind. He drank some more. Soon he had finished the bottle, and he threw it into the water. He started toward his horse, and he was staggering. Reaching the Appaloosa's side, he took hold of the saddle horn and lifted his foot, but he stumbled and fell. He rolled over in the dirt. He sat up slowly and cursed, and then lumbered clumsily to his feet. He went back to the horse and tried again. This time he managed to pull himself up and into the saddle.

He wanted some more whiskey, but he did not want to go back to Guadalupe. There was another town down the road— how far? He could not remember. He had passed through it on his way here. Well, no matter how far. He would go there. He rode, weaving in the saddle. He rode on, craving more whiskey. He rode on with the horrible image of the dying or dead man in his mind. He rode on toward whatever the hell the name of the other town was. He would get there. Sooner or later. He rode on. And then he fell out of the saddle and rolled over a few times, until he came to rest in the ditch beside the road. The big horse stopped. It walked over to him where he lay, and it nuzzled at him. Apparently satisfying itself that he was just asleep, it began to mill around on the side of the road. Slocum did not move.

When he woke up, he could tell by the sun that it was early morning. Slowly he recalled the events following the sloppy lynching of the night before, and he remembered wanting to get away from Guadalupe. He sat up and looked up and down the road. He did not think that he had gotten very far. He started to stand up, but he relaxed his body again and put a hand to his head.

"Oh," he said out loud.

He needed some coffee badly, and the nearest was back where he had started, back in Guadalupe, at Maudie's, or in the sheriff's office if he wanted to bother making it himself. He stood up slowly, and found his horse not far away. He climbed into the saddle and turned around toward Guadalupe. He rode slowly, and as he rode along, he recalled some of his thoughts from the night before. He recalled how he had wanted to get away from this place, but now in the light of morning of a new day, he rethought all of that. Not that Guadalupe was any more attractive than it had been the night before, but he recalled his promise to Cy Holbrook that he would stay and see this thing through.

Again he wondered how Holbrook might have handled himself in a similar situation. Would he have taken a chance on going down in a hail of lead? What good would that have done?

Damn all these promises anyway, he thought. He really would have ridden away from all this mess if he had not promised Cy. Well, if he had not worked awhile with Cy, making them partners in a way. He did want to find the culprit behind all this trouble, and he wanted to settle things down in Guadalupe again. He wanted to end the threat of a range war. He wanted Cy Holbrook to quit his job and get married and go to work out on the ranch. He wanted all of that, but, damn it, he wanted it to come about in a hurry. He really did want to get the hell out of there.

When he arrived at Maudie's, it was already late in the morning. There were no customers left in the place from breakfast.

He walked in and found a table. Maudie stepped out from the back room when she heard him come in.

"I need some coffee, Maudie," he said.

She brought it over to the table.

"Anything to eat?" she asked.

"No," he said. "Just coffee."

She stood looking at him for a moment.

"You want some company?" she asked.

"I won't be good company this morning," he said.

She pulled out a chair and sat down. "Times like that's when you most need company," she said. "I won't ask no questions."

16

Slocum rode out to the Zig Zag to see Holbrook, and he was
pleased to find the sheriff sitting up in bed and looking pretty
healthy. Slocum took the hat off his head as he entered the
bedroom. Holbrook grinned to see him.

"You're looking a little better," said Slocum.

"Well," Holbrook answered, "I'm hurting like hell, but I
guess that's the way I can tell that I'm still alive."

"I'm glad to see it."

Holbrook studied Slocum's face for a moment, and then he
said, "You got something on your mind, ain't you?"

"I hate to bother you with it."

"I can listen, and I can talk. Go on."

"I caught the son of a bitch that shot you," Slocum said.

"Good."

"But then I lost him."

"He escaped?" said Holbrook.

Slocum shook his head. "A mob out of the Hogback took
him out and strung him up. Right in front of me."

"My God," said Holbrook. "Did you try to stop them?"

"I tried," said Slocum. "Maybe I didn't try hard enough. I
didn't learn a damn thing from him either."

Josie came into the room just then with two cups of coffee.
She noticed that both men shut up as she entered. She gave
them each a cup and said, "It looks like I've interrupted something. I'll just get out."

They let her go, and then Holbrook said, "Well, hell, Slocum, I wouldn't worry too much over it. What's done is done. Likely you couldn't have stopped it nohow."

"What would you've done, Cy?"

Holbrook took a sip from his coffee cup. "That's hard to say," he said, "being as how I wasn't there. If I'd had a shotgun, I think I could have bluffed them all right."

"I didn't have no shotgun."

"They pull on you?"

"Yeah."

"How many was they?"

"Oh, I'd say about a dozen. Maybe more."

"Likely I'd've done just what you did. Like I said, don't let it worry you."

"Well," Slocum said, "it puts us right back where we started. The only two men we knew about are both dead now."

"Yeah. That's the tough part."

"What do we do?"

"Just wait, I guess."

Slocum made the rounds from the Circle X clear over to Roberts's spread. He rode slow and easy. He did not relish going back into town. The job was beginning to be frustrating, and more than a little embarrassing. After all, he'd had a prisoner taken away from him just the night before. He thought about going into Maudie's to eat, and into the Hogback for a drink, and he thought that he would almost for sure run into one or more of the men from the mob. He thought about the smug looks they would have on their faces. He was beginning to feel an intense hatred for them all. He had no other place to go, though, so he rode on back to town.

It was nearly lunchtime, and he had not eaten any breakfast that day. He was hungry, and so he forced himself to pull up in front of Maudie's. A crowd was already gathering in there, but he found himself a table. Maudie came around fairly soon, and he ordered a meal. While he was sipping coffee, he saw the cowboy who had furnished the rope of the night before come in and sit down at a table by himself. The cowboy shot a glance Slocum's way. After that he did his best to avoid Slocum's look.

Maudie brought Slocum's lunch, and while he was eating, she brought the cowboy's. Slocum finished eating and had another cup of coffee. He wasn't ready to leave just yet.

When he figured the cowboy was about done, he got up and paid for his meal. Then he went outside to wait. The frustrations from the night before were building up to an intensity inside him. In another few minutes, the cowboy stepped out the door. Slocum stepped behind him and shoved his Colt into the man's back.

"What—"

"Shut up and walk toward the jail," said Slocum.

"Now wait a minute."

"Move," Slocum said.

They walked to the jail, the cowboy's hands held high. Along the way, Slocum relieved him of his six-gun. Inside the jail, Slocum put the man in a cell and locked the door.

"What's this all about?" the cowboy asked.

"You know damn well what it's all about," said Slocum. "Lynching's against the law."

"I wasn't the only one."

"You ain't going to be in here by yourself for long," said Slocum. He went outside and sat down in the chair. He took out a cigar and a match and lit up, watching the clouds of smoke he puffed out. A man came walking down the street. Slocum recognized the man from the night before. He had been one of the mob. He was coming right at Slocum. As he got close, the man looked at Slocum and nodded his head. He appeared to be just a little nervous.

"Morning," the man said and walked on by. As he did, Slocum stood up and stepped behind him, poking his ribs with the barrel of his Colt and taking the man's sidearm out of the holster with his left hand. "Hey," the man said. "What is this?"

"Just turn around slow and walk into the jail," Slocum said. He marched the second man into the jail and put him in the cell with the other one. Then he went back outside and resumed his seat. He had left the front door standing open, and he could hear the conversation that was taking place inside the jail.

"What the hell does he think he's doing?" said the cowboy.

"Damned if I know," said the other. "Reckon he's planning to hold us for trial?"

"That'd be the dumbest thing he ever did. Hell, he couldn't get a jury from around here to convict us for lynching that son of a bitch."

"Well, he goddamn sure has disrupted my day."

"Yeah. Mine, too. Shit, I might could lose my job over this. I'm due back at the ranch in a couple of hours."

Slocum began feeling better. He sat in the chair for most of the afternoon just waiting for someone else to come by. By the time he was ready for supper, he had six men in the jail. No one else seemed to notice what he was doing either. He figured he had about six more to go. Maybe one or two more than that. He couldn't be real sure. By God, he thought, I'll get most of them. He knew that the men were right about the jury. He knew that in the long run they'd get away with what they had done. In the meantime, he would cause them some discomfort and inconvenience, and he would salvage his own reputation at the same time. He picked up one more on the street before he decided to go back to Maudie's for another meal.

He looked the crowd in Maudie's over carefully, but he did not see any of the other men from the mob. He sat down and ordered himself a meal. Maudie had it out to him in short order, and he ate with more relish than he had eaten his lunch. He was feeling better. When he finished, there was still a crowd in the place. He paid out, left and headed for the Hogback. He ordered a drink at the bar. He took his glass to a table and took a sip. He was positioned so that he could look the crowd over. He did not notice anyone from the mob. In another few minutes, though, the big man who had been the instigator of the whole thing came walking in with a strut. He went straight to the bar. Slocum got up and walked up behind him. He slipped his Colt out and poked him in the ribs, reaching for the man's gun at the same time. But the big man surprised him. He whirled and knocked Slocum's Colt out of his hand. Before Slocum had time to recover, the big man delivered a hard right to his jaw that sent him reeling.

Slocum shook his head to clear his brains. He looked at the big man, and the big man pulled out his own gun. Slocum stood still. The big man grinned and placed his gun on the bar.

"Come on now," said the big man.

Slocum doubled his fists and moved forward just as Amos said, "Hold on there. I don't want this place broke up. Take it outside."

Slocum picked up his fallen Colt and walked over to the bar, placing it beside the other one there. He looked at the big man. "Outside?" he said.

"After you," said the big man.

Slocum turned and walked out of the bar, the big man following him. Slocum stepped down into the street, and as he turned, the big man swung again. This time he sent Slocum sprawling in the street. Slocum wiped at his mouth with his sleeve and stood up. The man was tough. He had to give him that. Those first two blows, though, had both come as surprises. That wouldn't happen again. He moved toward the man. The big man swung another right, but Slocum blocked that one with his left arm and countered with his own right, catching the man on the jaw and staggering him. He followed immediately with a left hook that landed hard against the man's ear.

The big man covered his face with both hands, and Slocum began pounding him in the midsection. The big man staggered back with each punch. All of a sudden though, he seemed to get his second breath, and he shot out a right that sent Slocum spinning back. The big man was slow to follow up though. He'd had the breath pounded out of him. He stepped forward and swung another right, but Slocum managed to block it. Then the man kicked out with his right leg, reaching around behind Slocum and catching him at the back of the knees, causing him to fall into the street on his face. He rolled over quickly, but the big man was on him in a flash, sitting on his chest and choking him with both hands.

Slocum pried at the fingers, but he could not break their grip. His breath was cut off. He could feel his face puffing up. He kicked at the man's back and sides, but to no effect. He struggled, trying to roll over to either side, but the man's weight was too much to budge. Finally, he reached up with both hands and smacked the man hard on the ears.

"Ah," the man howled, and his grip loosened, and Slocum

slugged him in the side of the head with a fist. He slugged him again, and the man fell over to one side. Slocum quickly got to his feet, gasping for breath. He did not want to be on the ground again with the big son of a bitch. The big man got to his feet more slowly, and Slocum moved in, pounding his face and his gut with punch after punch until the big man fell to his knees.

"Have you had enough?" Slocum asked.

The big man did not answer, and Slocum stepped forward and delivered a deadly right to the side of the head. The man fell over sideways into the dirt. Slocum stood waiting for him to get up again. The man got to his hands and knees. Then he straightened up to just his knees. He brought one foot forward. He was about to get up, when Slocum hit him again, sending him sprawling back. Lying there in the street on his back, the big man held up his hands in front of his face.

"That's enough," he said. "I had enough."

Slocum pulled the man to his feet and started marching him toward the jail. In the jail, Slocum unlocked the cell door and shoved the big man inside. Then he closed and locked the door. The small cell was now crowded. Slocum put the keys in his pocket. He did not want anyone coming in and unlocking the cell again while he was away. He walked over to the gun rack and took out a shotgun. Checking it, he found it was not loaded, so he opened a drawer in the cabinet and found a box of shotgun shells. He put two shells into the gun and snapped it shut. Then he headed back for the Hogback.

Inside, he found the two guns still resting on the bar. He put his Colt back into the holster and tucked the big man's six-gun into his belt. Then he turned and looked around the barroom. He spotted two more of the men from the mob, and he headed for their table. Both men stood up with their hands in the air.

"We won't give you no trouble," said one of them. "We'll go along peaceful."

"Put your guns on the table," Slocum said.

The men eased their guns out and laid them on the table.

"Now step back."

As they stepped back, Slocum moved forward and picked up the guns. Then he motioned toward the door with the shotgun, and the two men started walking. In a few minutes, he had them in the cell. He locked the door again. He put the shotgun back in the rack and walked over to the table with the water pitcher and bowl. He poured out some water and washed his face. Then he dried it with the towel that was hanging there.

"Slocum," said the big man. "Why don't you let me have some of that?"

"Because I just don't like you," Slocum said.

"Well, can't you put half of us in that other cell?" said the cowboy. "It's pretty damn crowded in here."

"Do the best you can," said Slocum. "You've all been bragging about how you're going to get away with murder. No jury around here will convict you. That being the case, I mean to make you suffer as much as possible while you're waiting for your trial. And there will be a trial. I'm filing the charges."

"Ah, come on, Slocum."

"What's the point?"

"Let us out of here and there won't be no hard feelings."

"I've already got hard feeling," Slocum said. "And you ain't getting out."

"You can't just throw us in jail 'cause you don't like us."

"You're in jail because you took part in a lynching," Slocum said. "I can damn sure keep you in there on that charge. All I'm doing because I don't like you is making it more uncomfortable for you."

"I'm hungry. You can't starve us to death."

"I'll get someone to feed you soon enough."

He walked over to Maudie's and found her just about finishing up for the day. She smiled at him as he walked in.

"You got a mess of leftovers?" he asked.

"Yeah. I do."

"Enough for about a dozen men?"

"I think so."

"Well, throw it all together in a big pan," he said. "I got me a cell full of no-good bastards over there that say they need feeding."

17

For the next week or so, Slocum moped around, wishing that something would happen and longing for the time Holbrook would be up and about again. He picked up two more of the mob members and locked them up. The ones he had locked up first were getting very restless. Mostly he stayed away from the jail because of the noise. And they were beginning to smell a bit raunchy, too. He was sitting in Maudie's place one afternoon drinking coffee and visiting with Maudie when a young man came in.

"They told me that I'd find you here," he said to Slocum.

"What can I do for you?"

"I got a message from Geordie Gordon and his brother Pete."

"I don't believe I know them," said Slocum.

"Well, they was part of that lynch mob," the young man said. "In fact, I think they're the only ones you ain't got in jail already."

"Oh, yeah? Well, what's the message?"

"They said they was tired of hiding out from you. They said if you want them, you can find them at the old Meadows place. They'll be waiting."

"Yeah? When?"

"They're out there now."

"Is that it?"

"Yes, sir. That's it. Except for one thing. They don't mean to be brought in alive."

"We'll see about that," said Slocum. The young man left and Slocum finished up his coffee. He grabbed his hat and stood up.

"You going after them?" asked Maudie.

"That's right."

"What's the point? You said yourself no jury will ever convict those men."

"But they're going to spend some time in jail," Slocum said, "and they're going to face a jury."

"If they don't mean to be brought in—"

"That's their choice," Slocum said. "I'm going out there to arrest them. If they decide to fight it out, I can't help that."

He got directions to the Meadows place, an abandoned farmstead, and went to the stable to saddle up his horse. In a few minutes, he was on his way. He wore his Colt, and his Winchester was in the saddle boot. It was a ride of about five miles, most of it on the open road, but when he reached the fallen down gate to the lane that led up to the old house, he found the road tree-lined. He stopped at the gate and studied the trees for a time. He could see no one and detect no movement, but someone could have been hidden away in there waiting to shoot him from ambush. The two men he was after were ordinary citizens. He didn't really expect an ambush, but one never knew. He dismounted, took out his Winchester and slapped his horse on the rump.

"Go on, big fellow," he said. The Appaloosa trotted down the lane toward the house. Slocum moved into the trees. He worked his way slowly from tree to tree, keeping his eyes open for any surprises. By the time he had reached the trees nearest the house, he had found none. The Appaloosa stopped not far from the house. Slocum watched the door and the front windows. As he watched, he saw the ragged curtain on one of the front windows move aside just enough to allow someone to peep outside. At least one of them was in there all right.

"Hey, in there. You Gordons," Slocum yelled. There was no answer. "I know you're in there. I got your message. Come on out and there won't be no trouble."

"We ain't going to jail," came the answer.

"You're going back to town with me one way or the other."

"Come and get us then."

There was no easy way to the house. The space between the trees and the house was all clear, and the men inside would have a good view of him if he tried to make a run across there. And he had no target to shoot at. The men were in the house, but he couldn't see them. He had to start some action somehow. He looked around on the ground until he spotted a fist-sized rock. Leaning his Winchester against a tree trunk, he picked up the rock and hefted it a time or two. He decided that it would do just fine. Taking the rock in his right hand, he reared back and tossed it with all his might. It was a good throw, crashing through the front window on the left of the door, shattering the glass. Almost immediately there were shots from inside the house. None of them came too close to Slocum. Even so, he pressed his back against the far side of a tree trunk. He waited till the shots stopped.

Then he stepped quickly around the tree and fired a shot from his Colt. It went through the window, but it did no damage. He didn't expect it to. As soon as he fired, he moved back to the far side of the tree. Several shots answered him from the windows. He waited again before stepping out. This time he saw a figure at one of the windows. He fired, and he heard the man yelp and saw him fall away from the window. He could hear the voice from inside the house. "Pete. Pete."

Then everything was quiet again. Slocum waited, and in another minute, the front door was flung open and Geordie Gordon stepped out with a gun in each hand.

"Come out and fight, you son of a bitch," he yelled. "You've killed my brother. Where the hell are you? You dirty bastard. Come out and fight like a man."

Slocum stepped out in the open, his Colt in his right hand. He leveled it at Gordon.

"Drop your guns, Gordon," he said.

Gordon raised both guns and began firing. One bullet kicked up dust just a few inches from Slocum's right foot. He heard another as it whizzed by close to his left ear. He fired. His bullet smashed into Gordon's chest, and Gordon fell back heavily against the front wall of the old house. Slocum walked slowly toward him, keeping his Colt ready, but Gordon did not move. As he stepped up close to the body, Slocum saw the fingers relax and watched the guns fall from the dead hands. He picked them up and walked inside. The other Gordon was dead all right. Slocum gathered up his guns. He went back outside and walked around the house to where he found two horses tied. He put the guns in the saddlebags and led the horses around to the front. In a short time, he had the bodies loaded onto the horses. He caught up his own horse and mounted, and taking the reins of the other two, he rode back toward town.

It was late that afternoon when Slocum rode out to the Zig Zag to visit with Holbrook. He found the sheriff sitting up out on the porch. Josie was there, too, as was old Yates. They all stood up to greet Slocum as he dismounted.

"Come on up and have a chair," said Yates.

As Slocum climbed the stairs and took a chair, he jabbed a thumb toward Holbrook. "What's this?" he said.

"I tried to keep him down," said Josie, "but it was no use. He was wanting to ride to town today."

"That might be a little premature," Slocum said.

"Hell," said Holbrook, "I'm all right. I need to get back to work."

"I'd sure as hell welcome that," Slocum said, "but not till you're ready."

"I'm ready."

"Not till the doc says you're ready."

"Thanks, Slocum," said Josie. "I need all the help I can get to keep this stubborn jackass down."

"You want a drink, Slocum?" Yates asked.

"I wouldn't mind," Slocum said.

Josie stood up. "I'll get it," she said. She went into the house.

"Cy," said Slocum, "I got something to tell you. I got all those boys in jail now, except two. The last two decided they'd rather shoot it out than go to jail. I killed them both."

"Who were they?" said Holbrook.

"The Gordon brothers."

"Damn," said Holbrook. "They always seemed like pretty nice fellows to me."

"I wouldn't know about that," Slocum said. "They were two of the boys in that lynch mob, and they sent word in to me that they were waiting for me at the old Meadows place. I had to get directions to it. When I got out there, I asked them to ride back into town with me, but they decided to shoot instead. That's all I know."

"Well, I guess they asked for it," said Holbrook.

"Yeah," Slocum said. "Well, I'll be just as glad when you're back on your feet, and I don't have to make no more of them kind of damn decisions."

"Hell, Slocum, you're doing all right."

"I don't like it worth a damn. And besides that, you lied to me about that damned conscription. You was probably out of your fool head whenever you admitted it to me, but you did confess, and you told me that it was all a damned lie."

"I reckon I kind of remember telling you that. What if I was to say that I was lying that time?"

"That won't wash," said Slocum.

"No, I didn't think so."

"It was a dirty trick."

"I reckon so."

"A damn dirty trick, you son of a bitch."

"Well, hell, Slocum, I guess you can pull out anytime you've a mind to."

"That's a fine thing to say to me at a time like this."

"Like what?"

"You're all laid up and not worth a shit, and you've still got all this trouble around here. I can't run out on you now."

Josie came back out onto the porch just then. She was carrying a tray with a bottle and three glasses on it. She put the tray down on a table and poured three drinks, handing one each to old Yates, Slocum and Holbrook. They each thanked her, and Slocum said, "Ain't you having anything?"

"I'm going back in the house and leave you three to your men talk," she said. "I'll leave the bottle here."

Josie went back in. The men each took a sip of his drink. Holbrook said to Slocum, "So you ain't leaving me, huh?"

"No, not just yet anyhow."

"Well, I hate to break up your little confab," said Yates, "but just what are you two planning to do about all this trouble we been having?"

"Sim, I—"

"He ain't going to do nothing," said Slocum, interrupting Holbrook. "Not for a little while yet. In the meantime, the two men that we were sure were doing all the dirty work are dead. There just wasn't no helping it. We still don't know who it was paying them. So there ain't a damn thing we can do now."

"So that's it?"

"If we're right, then whoever we're after ain't got anyone to do the dirty work now. We'll have to wait till he hires someone else and they start in again."

"So we just wait till he kills another cowboy, huh?"

"We hope it won't come to that, Sim," said Holbrook.

"Yeah, but there ain't no g'arantees."

"You got any suggestions? We'll damn sure listen."

"Well, you can try to figure out who it is behind all this and get him before he hires any more gunnies."

"Mr. Yates," said Slocum, "we been trying to do that all along, but we just got nothing to go on."

"Just be patient with us, Sim. We'll get it done. I'll be up and out of here in another day or two. Then we'll really get busy."

"Well, all right."

"Wait a minute, Cy," said Slocum. "What do you mean when you get up and around, we'll get busy? What the hell will we be doing then, and how come I can't be doing it now?"

Holbrook leaned over toward Slocum and spoke in a soft voice. "Let's not argue here in front of ole Sim, Slocum. All I meant was that we'll have time to put our heads together and figure this thing out. That's all."

"Say," said Yates, "that looks like ole X. coming up the lane. What the hell does he want here?"

Slocum and Holbrook both turned their heads to look. Sure enough, X. Jones was riding toward the house. The men all stood up and waited for Jones to arrive at the porch.

"X.," said Yates. "What brings you around here?"

Jones dismounted and walked toward the steps.

"Come on up and set," said Yates.

"I just got back from the capital," Jones said. He sat down, breathing heavily. "Had some business to take care of."

"So how'd it go?" said Yates.

"Huh? Oh, it went just fine. But that ain't why I come over here."

"Well, I—"

"Oh, excuse me, X.," Yates said. "Can I get you a drink?"

"Yeah. Sure."

Yates got up and went to the door, opening it to yell inside. "Josie, would you bring another glass out here?" He went back to his chair to sit down again. In another minute, Josie came out with a glass.

"Oh, Mr. Jones," she said. "Welcome." She poured him a drink, excused herself and went back into the house. Jones sipped his whiskey.

"Now, X., what were you about to say?"

"Well," said Jones, "I heard some very interesting stuff while I was at the capital. Some of it might have something to do with what's been going on here."

"Well, stop beating around the bush and tell us," said Yates.

"The railroad's coming through here," said Jones.

"The railroad?"

"That's what I said. The railroad's coming, and it's cutting right through our ranches. Yours and mine. It'll run on through Guadalupe and out through the property of all the small ranchers. In another two months, there'll be railroad men out here to buy up all the property they need."

"What if we don't want to sell?" asked Yates.

"You know how the railroad operates," Jones said. "The government works right alongside them. They'll decide what land they need, and then the government will condemn it. They'll get it all right."

Yates was a little slow, but Slocum and Holbrook were looking at each other.

"So whoever it is we're looking for," Holbrook said, "somehow got advance word of this."

"That's sure what it sounds like to me," Slocum said. "He's trying to run off as many as he can, buy up the places and be ready to sell to the railroad when it comes through."

"Slocum," said Holbrook, "I think I ought to take a closer look at those land records."

18

Two days later, Holbrook was back in town. He was moving a bit gingerly, but at least he was up and about. It was afternoon when he reached town. The first thing he did was check the jail, and as soon as they saw him, all the prisoners started hollering at once. "Shut up," shouted Slocum.

"Let them out, Slocum," said Holbrook, "one at a time."

As the prisoners came out of the cell, Holbrook took down their names and returned their personal property. That was mostly guns. He told them to move over and stand against the wall and wait. When he had dealt with the last one, he stood up behind his desk.

"Now, listen to me," he said. "I'm going to get a court date set for your hearing. At a hearing, they determine whether or not there will be a trial. As soon as I have the date, I'll notify you. Now, this next is important, so pay attention. You show up at court the day of that hearing. If you fail to show, I'll hunt you up and put you right back in jail. You got that? All of you?"

They muttered that they understood, and hanging their heads, they shuffled out of the office, leaving Slocum and Holbrook alone. Holbrook went back behind his desk. "Have you had your lunch yet, Slocum?" he asked.

"No."

Crossing the street, Holbrook said, "You know, Slocum, I used to think that Maudie's cooking was just fine, but after eating Josie's meals out there at the Zig Zag, I don't know how good they're gonna taste anymore."

They went inside, and Maudie seemed genuinely pleased to see Holbrook up and around. She walked to a table with them and seated the sheriff. She inquired about his health and how he was feeling, and when she was assured that he was doing "pretty damn well," she got their order.

"I'll get it right out," she said. "Damn. It's good to have you back, Cy."

Holbrook looked at Slocum. "You haven't heard anything from out Roberts's way, have you?" he asked.

"Not a word."

"I sure would like to know what the hell's going on."

"My guess is that the man we're after only had them two working for him. They're both dead, so he's inactive. Till he replaces them."

"And we'll find out that the replacements have arrived when someone else turns up dead or some more cattle turn up missing," said Holbrook.

"Yeah," said Slocum. "That's likely the way it will be. Course, we can keep our eyes out for any strangers in town."

"Slocum, there's strangers in Guadalupe all the time. They come and go."

Maudie brought them coffee and went back to finish getting the meals together. Holbrook moaned slightly and stretched his upper body, wincing as he did.

"You hurting?" Slocum asked.

"Oh, a little. It comes and goes. I'll be all right."

Two of the recently released mob members came into the place and took a table across the room. They sat and glared at Slocum. Holbrook took note of it and said, "A couple of your new friends over there."

"Yeah," Slocum said. "I see them."

Maudie brought their lunches, and they finished them without incident, although as they paid and left, Slocum saw the two men still giving him mean looks. He didn't say anything to Holbrook, but he thought that they had not heard the last of those two, perhaps of the whole damn bunch. He walked over to the office with the sheriff, and he noticed that Holbrook was lagging a little.

"Cy," he said, "why don't you go in one of them cells and

lay down for a while. You look like you could really use a little rest."

"Hell, I ain't done nothing to make me tired."

"You made that long ride into town from the Zig Zag," Slocum said. "It's your first day out. You ought to take it easy."

Holbrook stood up from behind his desk. He took off his gunbelt and dropped it onto the desktop. "You may be right," he said. "I am tuckered out. Maybe I'll just take a short nap." He dropped his hat on the desk and walked into the near cell.

"I'll keep my eye on things," said Slocum.

"Thanks," said Holbrook, stretching out on the cot.

In a few more minutes, Slocum checked and saw that Holbrook was asleep. He went out of the office, closing the door easily as he left. He stiffened as he looked up and saw a rider in the street, a tall man wearing high-topped black boots with his black trousers tucked inside them. He wore a white shirt with a black vest over it, and he had a black string tie around his neck. His hat was black, too, wide-brimmed and flat. He sported a handlebar mustache, and on his hips were two matched revolvers in fancy tooled black leather holsters. As he rode past, the man looked directly at Slocum and nodded. Slocum reached up and touched the brim of his hat. The man rode on over to the hotel, dismounted, tied his horse at the hitching rail and went inside.

Slocum recognized Sam Giddings, a cold-blooded, professional killer of some wide reputation. He had seen Giddings once before, but they had never met. This could only mean one thing. The man that he and Holbrook were searching for had replaced his two dumb employees with Giddings. Slocum went back inside the office and around to the other side of the big desk. He pulled open a drawer and took out the stack of wanted posters he knew was in there. He went through the stack twice, but he found no sign of Giddings. It was what he had been afraid of. The man was not wanted for anything. There was nothing that he and Holbrook could do but wait for Giddings to make a move.

Perhaps that wasn't so bad, though, he thought. What they could do was watch every move that Giddings made and see if they couldn't catch him contacting his employer. After that, it wouldn't much matter how they handled things. They could just shoot the two sons of bitches down. What the hell?

Slocum wondered if Giddings had recognized him. He had certainly looked at him directly and nodded. If he did recognize Slocum, the last thing he would figure would be that Slocum was working for the law. Hell, it was the last thing Slocum would have figured. Giddings would probably find out soon enough, but before he did, Slocum might have a chance of learning something about him. He waited a little while, until he saw Giddings come out of the hotel and get back on his horse. Giddings rode down the street to the stable. In a few more minutes, he came walking out. He was obviously in town to stay a while. Slocum took a guess that Giddings would head for the Hogback next. It was the nearest of the two saloons. He decided to take a chance and headed across the street at an angle toward the place. He hit the batwing doors and went inside first, going to the bar and buying a bottle. He poured himself a drink and waited. In another minute, he heard the batwings hit. He glanced casually toward the doors and saw Giddings coming in.

Slocum turned away as if it were of no interest to him, lifted his glass and took a sip of whiskey. Giddings walked up to the bar and stood beside him. Slocum waited a few seconds before he looked.

"I saw you as I was coming into town," Giddings said.

"I know," Slocum said.

"You're John Slocum. I've heard a great deal about you. I'm—"

"Sam Giddings," Slocum said.

Giddings smiled. "So you've heard of me as well."

"I've heard some things. Can I buy you a drink?" Slocum held up the bottle by the neck.

"I don't mind," said Giddings.

"Amos," Slocum said. "Another glass."

Amos brought the glass and Slocum poured it full. He gestured toward an empty table. "Sit down?" he asked.

"Sure."

They walked over to the table, pulled out a couple of chairs and sat down facing each other across the table. Each man took a sip of his drink.

"Good whiskey," said Giddings. "Thanks."

"Where was it I saw you?" Slocum asked.

"If it was the last place I saw you," said Giddings, "it must have been El Paso."

"Yeah. That seems right. I was just passing through. You were—"

"Working," said Giddings.

"You just passing through here?"

"Working," said Giddings.

"Damn," said Slocum. "I didn't think there was anyone around here that could afford you."

Giddings chuckled. "I might not be as high as you think, Slocum."

"Oh, I expect I have a pretty good idea," Slocum said. "I don't suppose you'd tell me who hired you?"

"I can't do that."

"Or why?"

"I can't do that either."

Slocum shrugged. Giddings lifted his glass to take a drink but stopped. He looked at Slocum. "Say," he said, "are you working for anyone around here?"

"Not for near the money you are," Slocum said.

"Then it doesn't look like you and I will be facing each other," said Giddings.

Slocum shrugged again. "I guess you never know about those things," he said.

"Well, you can usually make a pretty good guess."

Giddings finished off his drink and held up a hand to stop him when Slocum started to refill it. "I've had a long ride, Slocum. I'm tired. I'm going over to the hotel, have a bath and then go to bed. Thanks for the drink."

"Anytime, Giddings," said Slocum. He watched as Giddings left the saloon. It won't be long, Slocum thought, before the son of a bitch finds out I'm working for the sheriff. It ought to get interesting after that. He drained his glass and poured it full again. Picking it up, he walked to the front window and looked outside to make sure that Giddings went straight back to the hotel. He did. Slocum finished his drink and took the bottle with him back over to the office. Holbrook was up and sitting at his desk.

"I got a tale to tell you, Cy," he said.

Slocum told Holbrook about seeing Giddings ride into town and about the conversation he'd had with the man in the Hogback.

"So," said Holbrook, "you figure he's the one that got hired to replace the two you killed?"

"It's got to be, Cy," said Slocum. "Who else in Guadalupe would hire Sam Giddings?"

"You're right about that," said Holbrook. "So what would you suggest we do?"

"Just watch him," said Slocum. "Maybe we can catch him meeting up with his boss. If we watch him close enough, maybe we can keep him from killing anyone."

"Or running off any cattle?"

"I don't think he'll do that, but whatever he might be fixing to try, if we're dogging him right enough, we can stop him. Whoever hired him on likely didn't count on me recognizing the man when he come riding into town."

"It's a good thing you saw him when you did."

"Lucky," said Slocum.

"He's in the hotel right now?"

Slocum nodded. "He said he was going to have a bath and go to bed. I watched him go in the hotel. I didn't see him come out again. Likely he was telling the truth. He didn't have no reason that he knew about to be lying to me, and he did not have a long ride to get here."

"We ought to keep an eye on the hotel anyhow," said Holbrook.

"I agree."

That evening Slocum stood in shadows watching the hotel. It was dark and it was late. There were few people on the street. He was craving a cigar and a glass of whiskey, and he was about to decide that Giddings was not coming out anyway, so he might as well go ahead, when the gunfighter came out the front door and stood for a moment looking one way and the other. Then he stepped on down and started walking along the sidewalk. Slo-

cum stood still. Giddings might be going for a drink. He was
headed for the Hogback. But he reached the Hogback and
walked right on past. Slocum got excited. He must be going to
contact his boss.

He waited a little longer, not wanting Giddings to spot him
and get suspicious. This was what he had been waiting for. He
was about to discover who it was behind all the trouble. It would
be a simple matter to wind everything up after that. He stepped
out at last when he was in danger of losing sight of Giddings,
and he started walking along the sidewalk, keeping close to the
buildings. It couldn't be much longer. There wasn't all that
much of town left that direction.

All of a sudden something grabbed Slocum by the collar and
pulled him between two buildings. His right hand automatically
went for his Colt, but someone grabbed hold of his wrist and
held it fast. He turned his head to get a look at whoever it was
who had grabbed him, but someone hit him alongside the head.
Then both of his arms were pinned behind his back. He struggled trying to shake off whoever was holding him, but a big
figure stepped up in front of him and drew back a fist. Slocum
tried to duck the blow, but he didn't quite manage it. It bounced
off the top of his head. Then someone took hold of him by the
hair of the head and pulled his head back, and he got a glimpse
of the man in front of him. It was the big man who had headed
up the lynch mob.

Then there was another man to his right, and that man dug
a fist into his right side. The big man hit him across the face
again, and then someone else drove a fist into his left side. He
took careful aim and swung his leg, delivering a brutal kick to
the big man's balls. The big man groaned and doubled up, and
Slocum heard the others curse and felt them pounding on him
even harder.

"You son of a bitch," the big man said, getting slowly to his
feet. He stepped in close and pounded Slocum's face over and
again with his big fists. At last, Slocum blacked out.

When he woke up, he could not move at first. He opened his
eyes and lay there on his back taking in deep breaths. At last
he moved, slowly and painfully. Everything hurt. He figured that
after he had passed out, they had kicked him in the head and in

the ribs. He managed to stand up, and then he staggered on out onto the street. He had no idea what time it was, but the streets were deserted. He staggered on over to the sheriff's office and found the door unlocked. He went inside, making much more noise than he had intended to make.

"Who's there?" he heard Holbrook call out from inside a cell.

"It's just me," said Slocum.

Holbrook got up and lit a lamp, and then he looked at Slocum.

"Jesus Christ," he said. "What the hell happened to you?"

"I lost Giddings," said Slocum.

19

Holbrook made Slocum sit down in a chair, and he got a wet rag and bathed his face. While he did, he kept asking questions. "Okay, so you lost Giddings. Now tell me the hell what happened."

"Aw, I was sneaking along the edge of the buildings kind of in the shadows, you know. I figured I had the son of a bitch. He didn't have much more of town to go. Then someone grabbed me from in between a couple of buildings, and before I knew it there were about five of them, maybe six, on me. They sure as hell beat the shit out of me. When I come to, there wasn't a soul on the street."

"I'd better get Doc to take a look at you," Holbrook said.

"No, hell, never mind that," Slocum said. "The worst hurt I got is here in my right rib cage. I don't know if they're broke or just bruised, but whichever they are, there ain't nothing ole Doc can do that I can't do for myself. All he'd do is just to tape them up."

"Shut up," said Holbrook. He walked over to his desk and got out the whiskey bottle and a glass. Walking back across the room, he handed them to Slocum. "I'm fetching him over anyhow. Have a drink while I'm gone."

Holbrook left the office, and Slocum poured himself a drink. He sure as hell didn't have anything else to do. God damn it, he thought, his ribs sure did hurt. The bastards must have kicked the shit out of him while he was out. Well, he had recognized the ringleader. That big son of a bitch. He would get him back for this. He promised himself. He was pouring a third drink when Holbrook came back in. Doc was right behind him. Doc examined Slocum carefully, but Slocum had been right. The worst thing he could find was the stove-in ribs. He wrapped Slocum around so tightly with bandages that Slocum could hardly take a deep breath.

"Take it easy now till they heal up," Doc said just before he left.

"Yeah. Sure." said Slocum.

"You better do what the doc says," Holbrook said. "Why don't you move on over into that cell and lay down on the cot?"

"In a minute," Slocum said. "Right now I'm finishing this drink. Listen, Cy, we might can pin this thing down. What's down there at the end of the street on the other side? Giddings was just coming even with Maudie's. What's left on that side of the street?"

"Well, Baker's office is down there."

"That shyster lawyer," said Slocum. "That's my bet."

"We need more to go on than your bet."

"Yeah, hell, I know. What else is down there?"

"Well, now, let's see. Hiram Miller's butcher shop. The stable. Blacksmith. That's about it I reckon."

"It's got to be one of them, Cy. What other reason did Giddings have for going down that way after dark than to see his new boss? I'll be watching again tonight, but this time I'll be a hell of a lot more careful about what's between the damn buildings."

"You'd better be. At least we've got it pinned down closer. Well, I don't know about you, but since there's nothing more we can do tonight, I'm going back to bed."

"Go ahead, Cy. I will, too, in a few minutes."

Holbrook went back into the cell he was using for a bedroom, and Slocum finished his drink and poured another one. Damn, his ribs hurt. Let's see, he thought, the damned lawyer, the butcher, the stable man, the blacksmith. Baker was still his first choice. In fact, he hardly thought about any of the others. He finished that last drink and decided that he was woozy enough. It wasn't really helping all that much with the bashed in ribs anyhow. They still hurt like blazes. He got up with a groan and went to the front door to latch it. Then he went into the other cell to lie down.

In the morning Slocum went with Holbrook to breakfast at Maudie's. They were early, so they were finishing as the crowd came in. Slocum saw the big man. His ribs still hurt like hell, but he wasn't going to let that stop him. He took a last slug of coffee to wash down his last swallow and stood up. The man saw him and stopped still. He looked deliberately away from Slocum to Holbrook.

"Morning, Cy," he said.

Holbrook just looked at the man. Slocum walked toward him. "I want you by yourself," he said. "Not with five or six of your cronies."

"What the hell are you talking about?" said the big man.

"You know damn well," Slocum said.

"I don't know what you want."

"Listen, buster, I recognized you last night. There's no question about it. You want to go outside with me right now, or you want to eat your breakfast first? I'll wait for you."

Holbrook stood up and walked over beside Slocum. "Hold on," he said. "I'm placing this man under arrest."

"For what?" said Slocum. "I ain't made a complaint. This is just between me and him."

The big man grinned. "Okay," he said. "If that's the way you want it, let's go on outside."

The big man turned and walked back out the door, and Slocum followed him. There were two other men with the big man, both of whom had been in the lynch mob, and Slocum figured that they, too, had beat him up the night before. He had not recognized them though, so he didn't say anything. He noticed though that they followed their big partner out the door. Holbrook followed Slocum, and about half of the people in Maudie's got up to go out and watch.

The big man walked to the middle of the street and turned to face Slocum, lifting up his fists and grinning. Slocum squared off, but Holbrook walked out to stand between the two. "Hold everything," he said. "Both of you take off your gunbelts and hand them here to me." He collected the guns and walked back to the front of the crowd that was by then gathered all around. Slocum looked at the big man's broad grin. The son of a bitch likely knows they stove up my goddamn ribs, he thought. He determined that he would not let the man know that his ribs were bothering him.

They moved in on each other and began circling slowly, each man looking for an opening. The big man, with the longer reach, shot out a few left jabs, but all of them were short of the mark. Slocum studied the jabs. When the next one came, he stepped forward quickly on his right leg and swung a hard right cross that caught the big man on the side of the head and made him stagger back. Slocum did not wait. He moved in fast, getting in underneath the long reach and pounding both fists one after the other into the man's gut. The big man staggered backward, but Slocum kept moving into him, kept pounding. The big man's fists flailed helplessly at Slocum's back. At last, Slocum backed the big man into the crowd at the far side of the street. A couple of men there held the big man up and forward, so his backpeddling came to an abrupt stop. Slocum kept pounding.

All of a sudden, Slocum stamped on the man's right foot as hard as he could. He thought that he could feel some little bones snap as he did, and the big man howled out loud in pain and doubled over. Then Slocum bashed him a hell of an uppercut that sent the man reeling back and over and into the arms of the men in the front of the crowd. He would have gone down, but they held him up. Slocum slugged him with a right cross and a left hook, and the man sagged in the arms of those who were holding him. Slocum backed off and looked at the man.

"Let go of him," he said.

They did, and the man fell forward on his face. Slocum walked over to the water trough and dipped out some water in his hands to splash his face. He was surprised at how good he felt. He still had no idea who the others in the crowd that had beat him were, but he just didn't give a damn anymore. This one had been the instigator. This was the big man. The others knew that if Slocum could whip the big man, he could whip each one of them easily. It was strange, but he was satisfied.

His ribs were hurting like hell though. He didn't let on. He walked toward the jail, and Holbrook followed. As he went past the unconscious man, the sheriff tossed the man's gunbelt onto his back. They reached the office and went inside, and Slocum looked out to make sure they had not been followed too closely. He shut the door, and then he doubled up in pain and groaned out loud.

"You damn fool," said Holbrook. "You sure you don't want me to lock him up?"

"What for?"

"Well, for assault and battery. For assaulting an officer."

"No," Slocum said between groans, "let's just call it even. You've got the son of a bitch and his pals all down for a trial for the lynching anyhow. Forget it."

"You are a damn fool. The doc told you to take it easy."

"Ah, shit," said Slocum, stretching and wincing. "God damn it, it was worth it."

Holbrook looked out the window and saw that much of the crowd was still out in the street, apparently talking about what they had just witnessed. A few were going back into Maudie's. Then he noticed that on the far side of the street, leaning against a post on the sidewalk and smoking a cigarette, was Sam Giddings.

"Slocum," he said. "When you can stand up straight again, come here and take a look."

Slocum straightened himself up and stretched, moaning at the same time. Then he walked over to stand beside Holbrook and look outside. He saw Giddings there.

"You suppose that son of a bitch was part of your audience?" the sheriff said.

"I never noticed," Slocum said.

"He looks plenty calm."

"Hell," said Slocum, "he's got no intention of fighting me that a way."

"Does he know you're working with me?"

"Likely he does by now," Slocum said. "He met with his boss last night and probably got told then. If he was out there watching just now, he seen me walk over here with you. I reckon he knows all right."

• • •

Later in the day, Slocum walked by himself over to the Hogback. He got a bottle and a glass and sat down at a table. He noticed that Giddings was alone at a table on the far side of the room. Giddings stood up and, bringing his glass with him, walked over to Slocum's table.

"Mind if I join you?" he said.

"I wish you would."

Giddings pulled out a chair and sat down. Slocum shoved his bottle toward the gunslinger. Giddings poured himself a drink. "Thanks, Slocum," he said. He lifted the glass as if for a toast and then drank. "Say, that was a hell of a fight you just had out there."

"Yeah?" said Slocum. "You were watching?"

"From the beginning. The other fellow had all the advantages. Height. Weight. Reach. You still whipped him, and you whipped him real good."

"Yeah, well, I had my reasons," Slocum said.

"I think I can see them," said Giddings, looking at the marks on Slocum's face. "How many were there?"

"Aw, I'd say about six. Maybe only five. I couldn't be sure. He was the only one I recognized."

"Well, I'd say you evened the score all right."

"I guess."

"By the way, you were holding out on me yesterday," Giddings said.

"I was?"

"You never told me you were working with the law here."

"Oh. That. Hell, you never told me who you were working for."

Giddings smiled. "No, I guess I didn't."

"Well?"

"I still can't tell you."

"You found out who I'm working for. We both know that we're on opposite sides. What's the difference?"

"The difference is that I made a promise. It's part of what I'm being paid for. I do the work and I don't tell anyone anything."

"You're a real honorable fellow," said Slocum.

"I have my code."

"I know what your job is, Giddings," said Slocum. "It's to run off as many ranchers as you can. Your boss, whoever the hell he is, means to buy up the property on account of he knows that the railroad is coming through. We got that much figured out."

"Pretty smart," said Giddings.

"So what I want to know is this. How do you plan on going about it? You going to kill a few more cowhands? I don't hardly think that rustling cattle is your style, but then, I could be wrong."

Giddings took a drink. "Slocum," he said, "you'll know what I'm going to do when I make my move and not before. I'll only tell you one thing. It will be perfectly legal. That's the only way I operate."

"No more drygulching, huh? No back-shooting?"

"None of that."

"I don't suppose you want to just go outside and shoot it out with me?"

"Not a chance."

"I know you ain't afraid."

"If I let you shoot first, you might get lucky," Giddings said, "and if I shoot first, I'll be arrested. There's no point. I can win my own way, and I mean to."

"Yeah? Well, I mean to stop you."

Slocum took out a cigar and lit it. As a big cloud of smoke rose up from the table, he picked up his drink and took a sip. Giddings took out his makings and rolled a cigarette. He struck a match and lit that. The two men sat in silence for a moment.

"You know, Slocum," said Giddings, "I like you. I think that I'm going to do this job without breaking any law, and I'll get paid, and I'll ride out of here without having to do a damn thing to you or about you. What do you think of that?"

"I don't think it'll work, Giddings," said Slocum.

"I wish you'd call me Sam."

"All right, Sam."

"Why don't you think it'll work?"

" 'Cause if you ruin these ranchers around here, I'll come gunning for you."

"That wouldn't be within the law."

"I won't be working for the law. I'll quit."

"Why do you give a damn? What's it to you?"

"Well, Sam, I've been around here for a while now, and I've made some friends. I like these folks, and I don't want to see anyone take anything away from them. If you do it, I'll kill you. Now, do you want to go outside and shoot it out?"

Giddings laughed. "Not a chance, Slocum. That was a good try, but not a chance." Slocum took a drink, and Giddings looked at him and smiled. "God damn it, Slocum, but I really do like you. You know, I don't believe you that you'll come gunning for me if I haven't broken the law."

"Don't bet your britches on it," said Slocum.

20

It was dark, and Slocum was walking back to the jail from the Hogback when a rifle sounded and a bullet kicked up dust near his feet. He ran like hell for the other side of the street and took a rolling dive for cover behind a corner in the sidewalk. After his roll stopped, he groaned from the pain it caused in his ribs. He eased the Colt out of his holster. Even that motion was painful because of the ribs. Who the hell had taken that shot at him? he wondered. It could have been Giddings, but he did not believe it. In the first place, Giddings was not carrying a rifle. In the second place, if it had been Giddings, the gunfighter would had to have gotten a rifle from someplace quick and then hurried outside after Slocum when Slocum left the saloon. The main thing though was that it just was not Giddings's style. Slocum's eyes roved up and down the sidewalk on the other side of the street, but he could not find any sign of the shooter.

He'd about had his fill of these back-shooting, bushwhacking, cowardly bastards around this town. Wasn't there anyone who dared to face a man? Well, damn it, he meant to get this one, whoever the hell it was. The world would be a better place without him. He studied the street, and he saw no movement. If there had been anyone out and about, the shot had scared them inside. Where was the son of a bitch?

The shot had sounded to Slocum like it came from the other side of the street and high up, like maybe the shooter was on top of one of the buildings over there. His eyes were scanning the rooftops, but he could see no one. He did not want to get up though and give the bastard a second chance. Then he caught a glimpse of movement from down on the street. He looked and saw Holbrook stepping out of the sheriff's office.

"Cy," he called out. "Get back inside."

The sheriff ducked back into the office just as a second shot rang out. It hit a few feet away from where Slocum lay hid. He had given away his position by shouting. He started scrunching backward in the dirt, until he had worked his way to between the two buildings there, and then he stood up. He moaned out loud because of the pain. Still he could not tell where the man might be hiding. He ran around behind the building and down to the far end of the street. Then he moved between the two buildings there till he was back at the street. If he was lucky, the shooter still thought that he was in the original place. He took a deep breath and ran across the street. About the time he made it, another shot was fired. The man had spotted him but too late to get off a good shot.

He hurried on around behind the buildings. There were three buildings with stairways on the backside. They all went up to second-story landings. There was no easy access to a rooftop. Maybe he was wrong about where the shots had come from. Maybe they had come from a second-story window, but he did not think so. He went to the nearest stairway and mounted the stairs. At the landing, he holstered his Colt and climbed up onto the rail. From there he could see over the edge of the roof. He did not see anyone, but he grabbed the roof anyway and wriggled his way up on top. It hurt like blazes. Then he pulled out his Colt again and started walking over the roof in a crouch. He had walked about halfway across the roof when he thought he saw a movement over on another roof, not the next one with a stairway, but the next one. It was four buildings down from where he was. He moved more cautiously, heading for the far edge of the roof at the front corner. The building was fronted by a facade that was like a wall from behind. Slocum hunched down behind it. He strained his eyes looking across three rooftops.

There was a man crouched there with a rifle. There was no mistake about it now. Slocum could not tell who the man was, but there was no question but that he was the shooter who had taken a couple of potshots at him. He raised his Colt, but he thought about it a second time. It would have been a long shot for a revolver. There was not much space between the buildings. He knew that he could make the jump. The question was could he make it quietly enough not to alert the man. Hell, he had to try it. He studied the roof of the next building. There was a tall and wide chimney poking out of the center of it. He would have to make for that.

He stood in a crouch and made a mighty leap, landing on his feet near the edge of the next roof and dropping almost immediately to his hands. He looked up quickly. The man seemed not to have noticed him. Staying in his crouch, Slocum walked hurriedly to the chimney. Now there was but one building between the two of them. He peeked around the edge of the chimney and saw the man moving. He seemed to be trying to locate Slocum down on the street. Slocum hurried on over to the far front corner of this building. He might be able to make his shot from there, but he didn't like his chances. It would be a lucky shot if it hit its mark. He did not like relying on luck. He would have to make another leap, and this time, surely, the man would hear him. Well, he thought, there is nothing else for it.

He backed away from the facade, crouched low, studied the distance and made the jump, landing as before on his feet but dropping quickly to his hands. He righted himself fast and looked and saw the shooter turn. He had heard him and he had seen him. Slocum ran, dived and rolled, and a shot sounded, a bullet plowed into the roof. Slocum scrambled to his feet and ran firing his Colt toward the man. The first shot went wild. The second hit the mark. The man shrieked with pain and surprise and tried to crank another shell into the chamber of his rifle.

Close to the far edge of the roof, Slocum stopped running. He held up his Colt and took a more careful shot. This one hit the man in the chest, dead center. The man jerked, stumbled back a few steps, lost his balance and fell off of the roof on the far side. Slocum straightened up. He walked to the facade of this roof and looked toward the sheriff's office.

"Cy," he yelled. "I got him."

He waited till he saw the sheriff come back out the door and look around.

"I'm up here, Cy."

Holbrook spotted him.

"You all right?" he yelled.

"I'm all right, but that back-shooter ain't. He's on the far side of that next building."

Holbrook started toward the body, and Slocum went to the back of the roof. He looked over the edge. There was no stairway on this one.

"Shit," he said. He got down on his belly and squirmed out over the edge, lowering himself until he was hanging from the eaves by his two hands. He let himself dangle there a moment, wincing from the pain in his rib cage, and then he dropped. When he landed, he doubled up and fell to the ground. "Ah," he groaned. He lay there in the dirt for a moment clenching his teeth and holding his sides. Then he stood up slowly, checked to make sure he had not lost his Colt along the way, and started walking toward where the man fell. As he rounded the corner of the building, he saw Holbrook standing over a body. He hobbled on over there and looked. It was the big man, the lynch mob leader.

"Damn," said Slocum. "Some men are never satisfied."

"He looks pretty satisfied now," said Holbrook. "I'll go get Riley."

Slocum had started back toward the office when he saw Giddings there on the sidewalk.

"Good job, Slocum," Giddings said.

"How would you know? I mighta shot him in the back."

"I saw the whole thing," Giddings said. "I came outside when I heard the first shot. I saw you run across the street, and I saw you jump from roof to roof. I saw it when the man turned on you with his rifle and you shot him. It was fair and square all right. It was a good job."

Slocum turned to walk away.

"But the man was no professional," Giddings said. "He was just a cowardly drygulcher. That's all."

Slocum stopped and turned back to face Giddings again.

"What was I supposed to make out of that?" he said.

"Nothing much. Just that you don't want to try to shoot it out with me like that. Remember that. I won't force it, Slocum. Don't you either."

Slocum and Holbrook were both sound asleep in the adjoining jail cells when someone came banging on the front door and screaming. They each jumped up, and Holbrook headed for the door to open it. Slocum grabbed his Colt.

"Fire," the voice shouted. "Hurry up."

Holbrook opened the door, and a man there said, "The Circle X range is in flames, Sheriff. I got to get all the help I can."

He ran on down the street. Slocum got into his clothes as quickly as he could, and Holbrook was not far behind him. Both men headed for the stable. In a few minutes, they were mounted and riding toward the Circle X. By the time they reached the Zig Zag, they could see a few of Yates's riders coming out to head over and help. They rode along with them. They could see the red sky ahead.

When they reached the fire, they saw a water wagon there. Men were soaking blankets and using them to beat on the flames. Other men were digging with shovels trying to create a fire break. Slocum grabbed a blanket and Holbrook took a shovel. Each man went to his own crew. The blaze was roaring, but the entire Circle X crew and apparently the whole crew from the Zig Zag were out, as well as a number of men from town. Slocum took note of how far from the ranch house the flames were, and he knew that if they did not stop it in time, it would take the ranch house out and then be on its way to the Zig Zag. He ignored the pain in his ribs and beat like hell at the fire. The heat was like a blast furnace, and the air was filled with choking smoke. Slocum beat against the flames until he thought that his ribs would crack open. He thought that his lungs would burst. He thought that the fight would never end, but at last it did.

They had stopped the fire, but the air was still heavy and thick with smoke, and the tired firefighters were hacking and coughing, picking up and loading their equipment, staggering from exhaustion and rubbing their stinging, red eyes. X. Jones found Sim Yates and shook his hand.

"Sim," he said, "I'da never made it without your help. Thanks to you."

"It's all right," said Yates. "You'da done the same for me. How bad do you think you're hurt by this?"

"It's hard to say. The sun'll be up soon. I'll ride out over it and see how bad it is."

"Just from what I see," Yates said, "you've lost a lot of grass. If you need it, you can drive your critters over on my range."

"Thank you, Sim. Thanks a lot."

With the job all done, Slocum began to really notice the pain again. He found Holbrook and walked over to join him. "How you feeling?" he asked.

"I thought I was all right as long as I was busy," Holbrook said. "I'm sure enough feeling it now though."

Slocum laughed. "I know it ain't funny," he said. "I know it because that's the way I'm feeling, too."

Both men laughed. They walked to their horses. Old X. Jones had already mounted up. He had named four men to stay out on the range and watch for any new outbreak. Then he hollered out for all to hear, "Come by the ranch house to rest up and get a drink and some breakfast. All of you."

Holbrook and Slocum rode to the Circle X ranch house and went inside. At first they drank water. Then they drank coffee. At last they had a drink of whiskey with X. Then breakfast was ready, and they sat down to eat. When they had finished, they got up to make room for more of the men, and then went out on the porch with another cup of coffee. X. came out to join them. They all found chairs and sat down. Even over at the ranch house, the air was smoky.

"I sure do appreciate the way everyone turned out to help," Jones said.

"Hell, X.," said Holbrook, "you know we wouldn't set on our ass in town while your place was burning."

"I still appreciate it."

"And I appreciate your good cooking and good coffee and—"

"Good whiskey," said Slocum. "I don't normally drink it this time of day, but it sure was good just the same."

"There's more," said Jones.

"No, thanks," said Slocum. "Coffee's fine just now."

"Sun'll be up in a few minutes," Jones said. "I'll be riding out to survey the damage."

"If you don't mind," Holbrook said, looking at Slocum, "we'll ride along."

"No, I don't mind," Jones said. "Does this mean you're suspicioning some meanness behind this?"

"With the trouble that's been going on, X., you never know. I just don't want to overlook anything. That's all."

"Why, if I was to think that some son of a bitch done this to me on purpose," Jones said, "I'd skin him alive and feed his carcass to my coon dogs. I'd—"

"We don't know anything, X. I just want to ride out with you and look around. That's all."

"Well, ride along and welcome."

They finished their coffee, and Jones went in the house to make his excuses to everyone and to tell them to stay as long as they liked. Then he went back out, and he and Holbrook and Slocum mounted up their horses and headed back out to where the fire had been. Jones halloed his four riders. They each said that everything seemed to be all right. As far as they could see, everything was black. They rode into it. At last they came to the far side. They rode onto good grass. They reached the place where the fire had started. There were no trees. No brush. They sat there staring for a few minutes. Jones was the first one to speak.

"It looks to me like I'll have to take ole Sim up on his offer," he said.

"What was that?" Holbrook asked.

"He told me if I had lost too much grass, to drive my cows over on his place. Looks like I'll have to do that."

"Yeah," Holbrook said. "It looks that way."

"It looks like something else to me," said Slocum.

"What are you talking about?" Holbrook said.

"Well, it's a clear night. No lightning. The fire started somewhere around here. That's for sure." He paused and looked at the other two men. The eastern sky was red and pink and purple along the horizon. Both other men waited for Slocum to continue.

"I just can't see any way in hell a fire would get started out here," Slocum said.

"I get you," said Holbrook. "Unless someone started it deliberate."

"That's right," said Slocum. "I'd bet my boots on it."

21

Slocum wrestled with his conscience for a long time following that night. He tried to talk himself into provoking a gunfight with Giddings. He could do it. He was sure of that. It would not be easy, but it could be done. There were several problems with the idea. The difficulty of provoking the fight was only the first. If he were to do it, it would piss off Holbrook almost for sure. He thought that he could manage to do it legally. Even so, it would be a deliberate killing. The worst though was that it would not help to locate the real culprit. Slocum thought that Baker was the man, but so far he had no way of proving that.

The other thing that was bothering him was the fire. He could not decide whether he believed Giddings had set it or not. It did not seem like Giddings's style. But who the hell else was there? It wasn't likely that the money man had done it. So far he had kept a really low profile, leaving no evidence of any kind to track him with. Did that mean that he had hired someone else? Some skulking little weasel of an arsonist? No one had seen anyone around the Circle X who did not belong there. Nothing suspicious had been spotted by anyone. Whoever set the blaze had been very careful going about it.

He was still puzzling over these things as he and Holbrook rode slowly back toward town. He glanced over at Holbrook and noticed that the sheriff was nodding in the saddle. Their sleep had been severely interrupted by the night's activities. He just might have a little nap himself when they got back to the office. Holbrook's head jerked and he came awake.

"God damn," he said. "I think I went to sleep."

"I think you did."

Holbrook yawned. "It ain't a bad idea except for I might fall out of the saddle."

"I don't know about you," Slocum said, "but I'm too damn sore to take a fall right now."

"Oh, God, yeah. This old body ain't been so tender in a long time."

"I'm going to try to catch Giddings again tonight going to see his boss," Slocum said suddenly. "Course, he might not do it. If he seen him already, he might not need to see him again for a while. But I think I'll watch for him again just in case."

"Well, that might not be a bad idea. You never know."

"Another thing," Slocum said. "I think I ought to ride out to see Roberts. Tell him about the fire if he ain't heard already. Those little ranchers ought to be setting night riders out to watch out for the same kind of tricks."

"That's a good idea," said Holbrook. "Let's just keep going when we hit town and ride straight out there."

"All right."

About the time Slocum and Holbrook rode through town headed to see Roberts, Burly Baker climbed into a buggy and drove out toward the Circle X. No one paid too much attention. And about the time Slocum and Holbrook arrived at Roberts's ranch, Baker was turning into the gateway that would lead him up to the Circle X ranch house. About half the crowd that had been out to fight the fire was gone, but there were still men being fed and plenty of men sitting around drinking coffee. X. Jones was in and out of the house, looking after folks' needs, thanking people for helping him out, giving instructions to cowhands. He had already told his foreman to get some of the boys, round up the entire herd and drive them toward the Zig Zag.

"Hell, Boss," the foreman had said, "ain't that sort a thing what caused some of them shootings?"

"Yeah, but this time Sim made me an offer. I mean to take him up on it, too."

Jones was about to go back into the house for some more

coffee when he saw the buggy coming. He stopped and studied the vehicle until it got close enough for him to recognize the driver.

"Now, what the hell does that damned lawyer want out here?" he said out loud but to no one in particular. The buggy pulled up in front of the porch and came to a rocking halt.

"Morning, X.," said Baker. "Sorry to hear about your bad luck last night."

"It wasn't hardly bad luck," Jones said. "It was deliberate."

"Are you sure about that?"

"As sure as you're a-setting there."

"Well, I am sorry to hear that, but I might have a solution to your troubles. I have a buyer who's interested in your place here. He'll make you a good offer."

"A buyer? Hell, I got nothing for sale."

"I hear you got no grass to speak of and you got a big herd. This might be a good time to count your losses and make a good sale. Hell, at your age, you ought to be thinking about retiring anyhow."

"Who is this damn buyer you're talking about?"

"I'm not at liberty to say, X., but he's serious. He's got the cash. What do you say?"

"I say this offer comes mighty close on the heels of that fire last night, Baker. Could it be that the two things is related? Could your buyer have known about that fire in advance? Maybe he had it set."

"Now, X., don't go jumping to conclusions. Everyone in town knows about the fire. He heard about it and thought you might be interested in selling. That's all."

"Well, I ain't, and you can go on back and tell him that. Besides, we all know about the railroad coming through now. If I was of a mind to sell, I'd just wait for them to get here. You wasted a trip, lawyer."

Jones turned and rudely walked away from the lawyer, going on into the house. Baker scowled and flicked the reins of the buggy. He turned it around and headed back toward town.

Slocum and Holbrook made it back to town in time for lunch at Maudie's. They found the place pretty busy, but they did find an unoccupied table and sat down. In a little while Maudie took their order. While they were waiting, Giddings came in. He smiled at Slocum, but Slocum just scowled. Giddings found a seat on the other side of the room. By the time Slocum and the sheriff had finished their meal, Giddings had just received his. No one had come in to sit with the gunfighter. He ate alone. Slocum wanted to stay and see if anyone would stop by to talk with Giddings. He decided that it was too much a long shot anyhow. The boss would not be seen in public with Giddings.

He decided to forget it. When Holbrook got up to pay, Slocum went with him. Giddings took his time with his lunch, and when he had finished, he had another cup of coffee. One and two at a time, the people left. Soon Giddings was alone in the place. After a few minutes, Maudie went to his table with the coffeepot and a cup.

"Some more?" she asked.

"Sure," he said.

She poured him a refill, and then poured the second cup full and sat down.

"I heard that X. Jones had a big fire last night," she said.

Giddings grinned. "I heard that, too," he said. "Too bad."

"I wonder if it hurt him bad enough to make him sell out."

"There's only one way to find out," said Giddings. "Make him an offer."

"I've already done that," she said.

Just then the door opened and Burly Baker came huffing in. "Maudie," he said, "I've got to talk to you."

"Go ahead," said Maudie. "You can talk in front of Sam."

Baker gave Giddings a look, and then he sat down. "Maudie, Jones won't sell. No one will now. Word's out about the railroad."

"Damn," said Maudie. "Who all knows?"

"I guess all the ranchers know about it. Jones said even if he was to sell, he'd just wait for the railroad to get here and sell to them."

Maudie stood up and paced the floor. "All that work for nothing," she said.

"You got that one place," said Giddings.

"Chicken feed," she said. "I've got to think of something else."

Giddings thought for a moment, considering his code. Desperate times, he told himself, called for desperate measures. "What if Jones and Yates were to just disappear?" he said. "Could you fake the papers somehow?"

"Now, wait a minute," said Baker.

"Oh, shut up, Burly," said Maudie. "I think you'd have to get rid of Slocum and Holbrook first. Slocum for sure."

"You want to play it that way?"

"I don't even want to know what you're talking about," said Baker. "All I've done is to act as an agent for purchasing land."

"It's too late now, lawyer," Giddings said. "You do know about it. I imagine that you figured it all out a while back anyhow."

"No, I didn't. Everything I've done is legal and—"

"Shut up," said Maudie. "I don't think I have a choice, Sam. They'll all put it together now. Hell, they'll get it out of Burly if nothing else."

"I won't talk," Baker said.

Maudie looked at him and smirked. Then she looked back at Giddings. "Take care of Yates and Jones," she said. "And there's that girl, Josie. She'll have to meet with some kind of accident. If she was still around, she'd question the whole deal. Burly, you work on the legal papers. Draw up deeds for both places. And find something with Yates's signature on it and something with Jones's. We'll have to forge the deed transfers. We've got to act fast now or it'll all be lost."

"What about Holbrook and Slocum?" Giddings asked.

"Yeah," said Maudie. "Yeah, get them first. Do it tonight. They're both sleeping in the jail."

"Well," said Giddings, standing up, "it's about time I started earning my pay."

Slocum was standing just inside the window of the sheriff's office when he saw Giddings leave Maudie's. He was thinking that the gunfighter had been in there for quite a while, when he saw Baker come out looking in both directions like he was afraid of being seen. So, he thought, Baker was in there to see Giddings. He had been right all along. He still had no proof, but he was convinced. Baker was the man he was after. There was no longer any question about it.

"Cy," he said. "Come here. Quick."

Holbrook jumped up from his chair and hurried over to the window. Slocum indicated Giddings, who was already some distance away from Maudie's. Then he pointed to Baker.

"They both just now came out of there," he said. "Baker was meeting with Giddings. Just like I thought."

"You're right," said Holbrook. "But we still have to come up with some proof."

"Why don't we just go see Baker and accuse him right to his face?" said Slocum.

"It'd be interesting to see how he reacts, wouldn't it?" said Holbrook. "Come on. Let's go do it."

They grabbed their hats and left the office, walking down the street toward Baker's law office. When they barged in, Baker came to his feet behind his desk. He was nervous and showing it.

"What can I do for you?" he said.

"You can tell us why you just had a meeting with Sam Giddings," said Holbrook.

"I never did. I—"

"We saw you and Giddings come out of Maudie's," said Slocum. "We've been trying to catch him meeting with the man who hired him to come here. It looks like you're it."

"Me? I never hired Giddings. I didn't go over there to meet with him either."

"What did you go for then?" Slocum asked. "I know you didn't go over there to eat. We left just a little while ago, and you weren't there. You went over there to meet with Giddings."

"No. I didn't. I . . . I went to see Maudie. I'm doing some legal work for her. That's all. Giddings was just in there drinking coffee. That's all."

"What kind of legal work, Burly?" said Holbrook.

"I can't tell you that. You know about a client's privilege. I can't tell you what I'm doing for a client. But I did not go over there to talk to Giddings. Now, if that's all, I have some work to do."

"For Maudie?" said Slocum.

"Yes. As a matter fact, it is for Maudie."

Holbrook looked over at Slocum. "Let's go," he said.

"The son of a bitch is lying, Cy."

"Come on," Holbrook said.

They left the law office and stopped out on the sidewalk.

"Why'd you let him off so easy?" Slocum asked.

"I didn't," said Holbrook, "but there's no way we can get him yet. He had all the right answers. Let's go see Maudie."

They walked to Maudie's and went in. There was no one around.

"Maudie," Holbrook called out. "You in there?"

Maudie came walking out from the back room. She looked surprised to see Slocum and the sheriff. "Well, hi, boys," she said. "What do you want? Coffee?"

"No, Maudie," said Holbrook. "We just came from Baker's office. We accused him of meeting with Giddings over here, and he denied it. He said that he came over here to meet with you on some legal matter. Is that true?"

"Why, yes, it is. He's doing some legal work for me."

"Can you tell us what it is?"

"I'd rather not," she said. "Do I have to?"

"No," said Holbrook. "You don't. Thanks, Maudie. Sorry we bothered you."

"It's no bother, Cy," she said.

Slocum and Holbrook left and went back over to the sheriff's office. Holbrook went behind his desk and sat down. Slocum paced and scratched his head.

"Cy," he said, "I know that damn lawyer was lying to us."

"Maudie backed up his story," Holbrook said.

"That's what's bothering me."

"What?"

"The other night just before that bunch jumped me, Giddings was on his way down the street. He was just about to Maudie's the last I knew. I figured he was on his way to Baker's office. Today I saw Giddings and Baker come out of Maudie's at just about the same time. It just makes sense that he was over there to meet up with Giddings."

"Well, yeah, but—"

"But he told us that he went to see Maudie, and Maudie backed him up."

"Right."

"Cy, what if we been on a wrong trail all this time? What if all the time we was looking for a man, we shoulda been looking for a woman?"

Holbrook stared at Slocum wide-eyed. "Maudie?" he said.

22

Baker went out the back door of his office and sneaked down to Maudie's. Looking both ways as before, he knocked on Maudie's back door. When she didn't answer immediately, he knocked again louder. At last she opened the door and he forced his way inside past her.

"What the hell's wrong with you?" Maudie said.

"Holbrook and that Slocum came to see me," he said. "They're on to us."

"Get hold of yourself. Just what did you tell them?"

"I didn't tell them anything, except that I was doing some legal work for you. I had to tell them that."

"That's all right. I know about that. They came here and asked me if it was true. I backed your story. So what's wrong?"

"I don't think they believed me, Maudie. I know they didn't. That Slocum told Holbrook right in front of me that I was lying. Holbrook made him leave. Slocum didn't believe a word I said."

"So you think they're on to us, do you?"

"Yes. Listen. We've got to get out of here."

"I told Giddings to take care of the both of them," Maudie said.

"What if they get him first? What then?"

Maudie began to feel a bit shaky. The damn lawyer was too squirrely. Even if her plans worked out, he could not be trusted. And he was right. Slocum might get Giddings instead of the other way around. It would be a quick short step to her then.

She had some money. She could get along without her property in Guadalupe. She decided that it might be best after all to just get the hell out while the getting was good.

"Go find Giddings and bring him around," she said.

"But I—"

"Shut up and listen to me. Go find him and tell him to get over here, but don't let anyone see you. And tell him the same thing. Now hurry up."

Baker hustled out the back door, and Maudie started changing her clothes. In a few minutes, she was dressed for riding. She rummaged through a chest and found a saddlebag, and then she rummaged some more. Pretty soon she had stuffed the bag with cash and a British Webley Bulldog pocket pistol. She was ready to go. There came a knock on her back door. She rushed over to open it, and Baker came in followed by Giddings.

"What's this all about?" Giddings asked.

"Baker says that they're on to us," said Maudie, "and I got to thinking, no offense, but what if Slocum should get you? I'd be out there all by myself. I'm getting out, Sam. Me and Baker. They've got us nailed. You riding out with us?"

"Wait a minute," said Giddings. "They can't arrest me. I haven't done anything."

"You started that fire."

"They can't prove that. You two go on and get out. Go to El Paso and stop at the White Hotel. I'll stay here and do the job you hired me to do. When I get all four men, I'll contact you, and you can come back."

"And if Slocum should get you—"

"You'll be away safe. No problem."

"The White Hotel in El Paso," said Maudie. "We'll be there. Come on, Burly. This could all work out after all."

Baker followed Maudie out the back door. Giddings went to the coffeepot and poured himself a cup. He sat down at one of the tables to drink his coffee. Maudie and Baker went to the back of the stable and acquired two saddled horses. They rode them out the back way. Baker was grumbling. He did not like horses. He wished they could have taken a buggy.

"They'd catch us for sure," Maudie said. "Shut up your whining."

Baker wanted to stop and rest several times, but Maudie made him keep riding until it was about suppertime. Then she stopped and made a camp. She fixed them something to eat. Baker started to fix himself a place to sleep, but Maudie told him to pack it up again.

"We'll ride as long as there's daylight," she said.

When suppertime came around, Holbrook and Slocum decided to go on over to Maudie's. They had not yet decided to confront her about their latest suspicions. As they stepped out the front door of the office, Slocum noticed people walking away from Maudie's shaking their heads. One man who was headed for the place was stopped by another who was coming out. Holbrook hailed the man who had done the stopping and he walked over to the office.

"What's going on over there?" Holbrook asked.

"Hell, I don't know. I went over there to get some grub like usual, and when I went inside there wasn't no one in there but that gunfighting fellow, you know."

"Giddings?" said Slocum.

"Yeah. He's just sitting in there all by his lonesome sipping at a cup of coffee. When I walked in, he said to me, 'Maudie's is closed, partner.' That was all he said."

"Thanks," said Holbrook.

As the man went on his way, Holbrook and Slocum gave each other a look.

"What do you make of it, Cy?" Slocum said.

"Giddings is up to something."

"Yeah. But what?"

"You want to go over there and find out?" Holbrook said.

"He could be just sitting there waiting for us to show up," Slocum said. "If we walk through that front door, he could kill one of us for sure."

"Well, what do we do then?"

"I think I'll just sit out here on the sidewalk and smoke a cigar," Slocum said.

"What?"

"If he is waiting for us, he'll get impatient after a while. He'll have to come to the door and look out."

He walked to the cell where he had been sleeping and got his Winchester. Holbrook eyed him with curiosity. Slocum walked over to the gun rack and took out another rifle, which he handed to Holbrook.

"If we can keep him out of the range of his six-guns, we'll have a better chance," Slocum said. "He might figure that out if he looks over here and sees me with this Winchester. I'd suggest that you take this one around to the back of Maudie's, but stay well back."

"Out of his range," said Holbrook.

"That's right."

Slocum fished a cigar and a match out of his pocket. He struck the match and lit the cigar. Then he walked outside and took the chair out there. He leaned his Winchester against the wall. Maybe Giddings would not notice it. Holbrook followed Slocum outside, but he kept walking. When he was a good ways down the street, he crossed it and went between two buildings. Slocum puffed his cigar and watched the front of Maudie's. About half of his cigar was gone when he saw the front curtain of Maudie's move. Giddings was looking out. In another few minutes, the gunman stepped out the front door. He stood in the doorway looking across the street at Slocum. Slocum tipped his hat.

"Slocum," Giddings called out. "You coming over to supper?"

"I heard the place was closed," Slocum said.

"It's not closed to you. Come on over."

"I ain't hungry just now."

"Aw, come on. I'm buying."

"No thanks, Giddings. I like to choose my dinner company."

"Hey, you and me are two of a kind. A real pair. Come on over and eat with me."

"I don't think so."

Giddings walked out from the doorway a few steps, and Slocum noticed that he tested the looseness of his revolver in the holster. He had to come closer to get a good shot. Slocum let him walk a little closer but still not close enough. He reached back and picked up the Winchester, laying it across his knees. Giddings stopped.

"What's that for?" he said.

"It's for you, Giddings. Keep coming."

"I didn't expect that from you."

"What's wrong, Giddings? You were asking me over just a few minutes ago. Now you won't cross the street to see me."

Slocum lifted the rifle and cranked a shell into the chamber. Giddings walked back a few steps. Slocum raised the rifle, and Giddings turned and ran back into Maudie's, a rifle shell smashing into the door frame just behind him. "Damn," he said, and he ran to the back door. He jerked it open, and a rifle bullet whizzed past his head, breaking a picture that was hanging on the wall. He slammed the door and latched it. He went back to the front door and opened it carefully.

"Slocum," he called out.

"What do you want?"

"Put down that rifle and I'll come out and face you fair and square."

"Not a chance."

"You've got me pinned in here with two rifles."

"Pretty smart, wouldn't you say?"

"Damn it, Slocum, you can't do this. I haven't broken any laws in this town."

"We know you were working for Maudie," Slocum said. "And we know what she was doing. We've got several killings chalked up to her. Not to mention some cattle rustling and setting a fire."

"I wasn't even here when those killings took place."

"You're working for her."

"Not anymore. Hell, she's left town. With that lawyer."

That came as a surprise to Slocum, but he did not let on. "Toss out your guns and you can come out," he said.

"Not a chance."

"Suit yourself. I reckon you'll get tired of sitting in there all by yourself in a short while."

Giddings shut and latched the front door. He was caught in a trap, and he did not like it. He looked all through the place, but he could find no rifle. Neither could he find a window other than the front one. There was no way out. He tried to come up with a plan, but the only thing that he could think of was to fling open a door and run for cover, try to get close enough to one of them to shoot with his six-gun. It was not a good plan. He went to the back door again and opened it a crack. Peering out, he could not locate the other man. He assumed it was Holbrook. He could not find any cover out there either. He shut the door and latched it again.

He went to the front window and looked out. There was a watering trough out there, but it would be a good run to get to it, and he wasn't sure he could get a good shot from there anyhow. Yes, he was trapped like a rat. What if he gave himself up? Could they really pin those killings on him just because he was working for Maudie? He wasn't sure. He'd be taking a hell of a chance. Standing to one side of the window, he reached over and shoved it up a crack.

"Slocum," he yelled.

"What is it?"

"Slocum, let me walk out of here, and I'll just leave town. You won't see me back here. What do you say?"

"I don't think so, Giddings," Slocum said. "I don't trust you, and right now, I've got you where I want you. I think we'll just keep things the way they are."

"You son of a bitch."

Giddings wracked his brain, but he could not come up with anything new. Well, there was nothing for it but to go out shooting. He was good with his six-guns. He knew that. He knew *how* good he was, too. If he went out blasting, there was a chance he could get Slocum before Slocum could get off a shot with that damn rifle. He would have to try it. He went to the door again. He unlatched it. He swung it open. He drew out both his revolvers, and he ran outside at once. He ran straight toward Slocum shooting both guns.

Slocum jumped to his feet and raised the rifle to his shoulder. One of Giddings's bullets nicked his ear. He aimed and fired, and his bullet tore into Giddings's right shoulder, spinning him around. He stayed on his feet though and, staggering, lifted his left-hand gun. Slocum cranked another shell into the chamber. Giddings was still staggering, and his shot was off. Slocum fired again. This shot knocked Giddings over backward. Slocum started walking toward Giddings. The man was not quite dead, and he still held a gun in his left hand. He was still dangerous.

Down the street, Holbrook came running from between two buildings. He stopped when he saw Slocum walking toward the prone Giddings. He, too, walked. Slocum got to Giddings first, and he reached out a foot and kicked the gun away from Giddings's left hand. Giddings rolled his eyeballs to look at Slocum. He was breathing heavily.

"Slocum," he said.

Holbrook walked up just then. "Good work, Slocum," he said. "You got him."

"It took both of you," said Giddings, panting.

"You're just as dead, Giddings," Slocum said. "You should've tossed out your guns."

"Not likely," said Giddings, and then his eyes went blank. He stopped breathing. He was dead.

"Well, that's a relief," said Holbrook. He looked up and saw Riley peeking out his door. Holbrook waved the undertaker on over. "Send me the bill," he said. He picked up Giddings's two guns and started walking to the office. Slocum followed him.

"He told me that Maudie and Baker had left town," Slocum said.

"We can check at the stable," said Holbrook. "It's the only way they could've gone."

"We can't let them get away."

"I can get a posse together."

"No. One man'll be enough. I'll go after them."

"I can ride with you," said Holbrook.

"I don't think you're yet up to a long ride," Slocum said. "Besides, if you go, the town'll be without a lawman. I'm still a deputy, ain't I?"

"Well, yeah, I reckon you are."

"Then tell me to go get them."

"Slocum," said Holbrook, "go get them. Bring them back alive if you can."

"I'll do my damndest."

23

Slocum left town tracking Maudie and Baker, and Holbrook decided to ride out to the Zig Zag with the latest news. He left his horse in front of the porch and climbed up to knock on the door. It was opened by Sim Yates, and as Holbrook walked in, Josie stepped out of the kitchen to see who had come.

"Hello, Cy," she said. She walked across the room to give him a hug, and old Yates noticed the affection with which it was done. He figured that something had developed between the two of them while the sheriff had been convalescing at his home. It was all right with him. He liked Holbrook.

"What brings you out this way?" the old man asked.

"I've got some news," said Holbrook. "I wanted you two to be the first to hear it."

"Well, out with it, boy," said Yates. "Is it good or bad?"

"It was Maudie who hired Giddings and those other boys. She was hoping to buy up enough property around here to make a killing when the railroad comes through."

"Maudie?" said Josie. "Why, that's almost unbelievable."

"She and Baker were working together," Holbrook went on. "They hightailed it out of town when we caught on. Left Giddings in her eating place. I guess he was supposed to get me and Slocum. Then he was likely coming after you folks. Anyhow, Slocum killed him and then took out after Baker and Maudie. It's just about all over, folks."

"My God," said Yates. "That's good news."

"Course," said Holbrook, "the town'll be without a lawyer now."

"That might be the best news yet," said Yates. "Say, I have an idea. Why don't we throw a shindig out here. Invite X. and his whole crew. Even Roberts and that bunch. You can make the announcement then to everyone at the same time."

"That's a wonderful idea," Josie said. "It would be a good place to make all kinds of announcements." She gave Holbrook a lingering look. The sheriff fooled with the hat that was in his hands, looked at the floor and shuffled his feet.

"We'd ought to wait for Slocum to get back," he said.

"Let's have it a week from tonight," said Yates. "Hell, the word'll leak out by then, so we can go on ahead and tell them what's happened and what's the purpose of the party. It'll be a hell of a good time."

"Yes," said Josie.

"I'll send Loy and Mac out to spread the word and make the invites," Yates said. "That'll save you some riding, Cy."

"I appreciate that, Sim. Well, I guess I'll head back for town."

He walked back to the door and hesitated. Then he turned around again and looked at Josie. "Josie," he said, his face red as a beet, "could I talk to you alone for a minute?"

"Well, yeah," she said. "You want to go out on the porch?"

"I'm going out," said Yates. "You two'll be alone in here."

The old rancher got up, put on his hat and went outside. Holbrook stood looking stupid. Josie walked over to him.

"You want to sit down, Cy?" she said.

"No," he said. "I think I'd better not. I'll just stand here if it's all right."

"All right."

"Josie, as soon as Slocum gets back and this ugly business is all wrapped up for sure—"

"Cy, nothing about you and me has anything to do with this ugly business. If you've got something to ask me, just go ahead and ask it."

"But I'm a sheriff, Josie, and—"

"I don't give a damn what you are."

"Well, I can't—"

"Then I guess I'll have to do it. Do you want to marry me, Cy? Is that what we're talking about here?"

"Well, yes, I—"

"Then let's just go on and do it."

"You mean—"

"Let's do it right now. Or just as soon as we can make it legal. Let's go into town and see the preacher. We don't need a big wedding. A small quick one will last just as long. What do you say, Cy? I'm ready if you are."

Slocum was pursuing an unpleasant task. He had to bring in the two fugitives, but he had never before chased down two such as these. One was a woman, a woman he had made love to. He had liked Maudie. At least, he'd thought he had liked her. It had become obvious that he had never really known her. He wished that there had been someone else to run them down, but he was the only one. Holbrook was still too weak from his gunshot wound to make a chase like this. They were headed into the mountains, so it looked like it could be a rough ride. It was late in the day, too. It might involve at least one overnight camp. He also did not like the idea of shooting a woman, and he hoped that Maudie would not give him any problems.

Then there was Baker. Slocum had no liking for Baker, but Baker was a fat wretch, a man the killing of whom would bring no real satisfaction and certainly no sense of pride. Killing Baker would be like shooting a helpless dog. Even worse. Slocum thought that if he could manage to sneak up on the two of them and get the drop on them, they would give up. He could take them back to stand trial. Once he had done that, he would be free to get the hell away from Guadalupe. He was anxious for that day. The sun was low in the sky, and he knew that he would not be able to ride much longer. He started watching for a good campsite.

"Maudie," said Baker, "we have to stop. It'll be dark soon, and we can't ride out here in the darkness. This damn horse is killing me anyway. I need to stop."

"All right," she said. "We'll stop up ahead. Cut out your damn whining."

They rode on for a ways, and then they came to a sheltered spot at the base of a hill. There was no water around, but Maudie had brought along several canteens. She stopped her horse and dismounted. "This ought to do it," she said. Baker almost fell off his horse. He moaned as his feet hit the ground, and he staggered over to sit down heavily on the ground.

"Hey," Maudie said, "you've got to get the saddle off that horse. Get your fat ass up and take care of it."

Baker groaned more as he lumbered back to his feet. He walked back to the horse and started to unsaddle it. Maudie had hers taken care of, and she started gathering sticks for a fire. Soon she had coffee making. She busied herself then with some food she had packed. They would have a good meal in just a few minutes. Maudie was not happy with her company. She had never liked Baker, but as he was the only lawyer around, she had found it necessary to work with him. It had never occurred to her that she would be in a situation like this with the man. Now the only reason for keeping him around was in case Giddings got the job done. Then they would need Baker to forge the documents and finalize the phony sales.

"I can't believe I let myself get drawn into this mess with you," Baker said.

Maudie turned on him.

"What the hell are you talking about?" she said.

"Look at us," he said. "Running away like common criminals. I left my office, my practice back there. I left money in the bank. What if Slocum does kill Giddings? What then? We can't go back to Guadalupe. Not ever. What will I do?"

"I walked away from everything, too, you whimpering little shit," Maudie said. "That kind of talk won't get you anywhere. I sure ain't feeling sorry for you. And what if Giddings gets Slocum? Huh? Think about that. We'll go back to Guadalupe and get rich as hell. That's what you took this chance for, ain't it? You greedy bastard. You're as greedy as I am, and you came into this with your eyes open. So shut the hell up about it."

Angrily, she dished out some food and handed a plate to the fat lawyer. He took it and ate like it might be his last meal. Maudie fixed herself a plate and sat down to eat. There was no more talking. When they finished their meal, Maudie cleaned the dishes as best she could with sand, and they drank coffee. Baker was surly. There was still no talk. Maudie decided there would be no breakfast in the morning. No coffee even. They would get up early and hit the trail. Fuck Baker and his whining. She was sick of it. She made herself a place to sleep and let the sorry ass lawyer fend for himself. As she stretched out on the ground, she smiled a bit to herself as the nearly helpless man struggled to fix himself a bed. Finally he was lying down, but he moaned and groaned so much that Maudie had a hell of a time getting to sleep.

When she woke up in the morning, the sun had not yet shown itself, but it was beginning to light the far eastern horizon. She was ready to go. She could hear the lawyer still snoring. She started to kick him to wake him up, but suddenly she realized that there was only one horse. She started to panic. Then she calmed herself down. Baker's horse was gone. The son of a bitch had not secured it the night before. Well, that did it. As quietly as she could, she packed up and saddled her horse. She took one last look at the snoring wretch. He had taken off his jacket and laid it out beside him. His wallet was in that jacket.

Slowly and carefully, she walked over to the jacket and picked it up. She felt for the wallet and found it. Dropping the jacket on the ground, she opened the wallet and pulled out all the bills she found in there. Then she dropped the wallet on the coat. She moved quietly to her horse, mounted up and rode slowly away. Baker was still sound asleep.

The sun was completely visible over the horizon when Baker finally stirred. He rolled over, rubbing his eyes and moaning out loud. He was hoping that Maudie had the coffee ready. He sure could use some. And breakfast. He thought that he could have done a lot worse than run away with a good cook. With a loud grunt, he sat up and looked around. He was alone. Maudie was gone with both horses. His saddle was still there, but that was all. Well, there was his jacket, but something was wrong there, too. He saw the wallet lying loose on top of the rumpled jacket, and he reached for it desperately, looking inside. The money was gone. It was everything he had.

"Maudie," he called out, but there was no answer. He stood up and turned in circles looking in every direction. Damn her, she had robbed him in the night. "Maudie?" Maybe it was just a cruel joke, and she would return in a few minutes laughing at what she had done. He looked around some more. She had taken everything. There was no food, no coffee, not even water. What the hell did she think? Did she think that she did not need him anymore? She would not be able to handle the legalities of this complicated deal. Only he could do that. She was a fool. A damned fool.

Something was wrong. She must be just around the bend. He turned around again, looking in all directions, but he saw no sign of her, and all of a sudden, he realized that he did not know in which direction they had been traveling. A high hill rose just behind him. He thought that he would be able to spot her from up on top of it. He started to climb in desperation. Twice along the way, his foot slipped and he slid back down to the place he had started from. The knees were ripped out of his trousers. His shirt was torn. His hands were bleeding. He started to cry. But at last, he reached the top of the rocky hill. He stood up and looked all around.

Still he could not see her. He dropped heavily to his fat ass, and the rocks hurt him when he landed. He started to sob. He lifted his head to take a deep breath, and then he spotted her. She was just riding up out of a ravine. He stood up, reaching out toward her. "Maudie," he called out, but she did not show any sign of having heard him. She just continued riding away. "Maudie," he screamed in desperation. He ran toward her, calling her name. "Damn you," he shrieked at last. "Damn you. You can't do this to me." He came to the edge of the hill, and the rocks beneath his feet gave way. His feet shot out in front of him, and he landed hard on his ass and started to slide. He screamed. He tried to stop himself. After a little ways, he caught a solid boulder with his foot, but his momentum was just too much. He did not stop. Instead, he flipped over, landing on his face and belly, and he continued to slide and tumble down the hillside. He was almost to the bottom of the hill, when he flipped again. This time his head struck hard against a rock. When he finally stopped sliding, he lay still, his head in a widening pool of blood.

• • •

Slocum had started the day early, but he had fixed himself a breakfast and some coffee. He had cleaned up his campsite, saddled his Appaloosa and gotten back on the trail. The trail was not hard to follow. He knew that he was moving alone right behind them. Hell, he thought, a gal and a citified lawyer wouldn't be hard to track and to catch up to out here. It was about mid-morning when he saw the stray horse. He caught it up with little trouble. It was wearing a harness but no saddle. He caught up the reins, which were trailing, and he noticed the brand. It belonged to the stable back in Guadalupe. He had checked there before leaving town and learned that Maudie and Baker had hired horses. He did not bother telling the stable man that they probably had no intention of returning them. Holding the reins of the stolen horse, he continued on the trail.

It wasn't long before he saw something on the ground near the base of a hill. He rode toward it. As he got closer, it looked like a campsite that no one had bothered to clean up. But there was something on the ground there. He rode on over and dismounted, and he found Baker's jacket, wallet and a saddle. That was curious. The saddle had to have come from the horse that he had already picked up, but why was the jacket left behind? And the wallet had no cash in it. Why would Baker leave his wallet, cash or no? Slocum secured both horses and continued to look around. He was walking around the bottom of the hill when he found Baker's body. He examined it carefully. It sure as hell looked like the man had fallen down the side of the hill. The back of his skull was cracked. It looked like he had hit it on a rock. But why had the silly son of a bitch climbed up to the top of the hill in the first place?

Slocum considered the possibilities. Perhaps the two had split up, thinking that they would have a better chance of eluding any pursuit that way. Then Baker had fucked up somehow, lost his horse and climbed up the hill, looking around, trying to get his bearings or find his stray horse or something. It could have happened that way. But what about his wallet? There was no money. Slocum thought it more likely that Maudie had tired of the man and left him behind, emptying his wallet in the process. She had not killed him. It didn't seem so. So she had likely simply slipped away from him in the night or the early morning.

Then the poor bastard had climbed the hill trying to spot her, and somehow, he had slipped and fallen. That seemed to be the most logical choice.

Slocum was a bit surprised at the cold-bloodedness of Maudie. It was a cruel thing to leave a man stranded in country like this. Then he thought that he should not be surprised though. After all, she'd had men murdered. She had tried to have Holbrook and Slocum killed as well. He guessed that he was still somehow trying to come to grips with the notion of Maudie as the head of all this shit. He walked back around to the campsite, picked up the saddle and put it on the stolen horse. Then he mounted up and, taking the reins of the extra horse, started on the trail again.

24

It was past noon. Maudie could tell by where the sun was in the sky. She was hungry. She had started the day with no breakfast and no coffee even. She thought that she was well enough ahead of any pursuit to allow herself the leisure of a quick camp and a meal. She stopped in a little valley and gave the horse some water. She still had plenty. Then she built up a small fire and put the coffee on to boil. She took out some of her trail food and started to prepare a meal. In a few minutes, while the food was still cooking, she poured herself a cup of coffee and sat down to drink it. It surely did taste good. At times like this, she told herself, a person was grateful for simple pleasures.

She thought about her situation, and she wondered what had happened back in Guadalupe. If Giddings had been successful, he would soon meet up with her in El Paso. They would have to figure out how to deal with the paperwork without Baker, but that shouldn't be too much of a problem. Everything would work out after all, just the way she had planned it. She would have all the money she needed. At least for a while. She still had a pretty good ride ahead of her. Well, she'd be done here soon and get back on the trail. She would make that trip in good time. She wondered just what she would tell Giddings when he asked her about Baker. She might just tell him the truth. It didn't matter much. She stiffened all of a sudden when she heard a noise behind her, the sound of footsteps. She started to turn her head for a look.

"Just sit still, Maudie," came a voice. She recognized it as Slocum's. God damn, she thought. She relaxed a bit and took a sip of her coffee.

"Slocum?" she said. "That you?"

"It's me."

Slowly, she turned her head to see him walking down the hillside, coming toward her. He had his Colt in his hand, and it was pointed at her back.

"Welcome, honey. Where's your horse?" she asked.

"I left him up on the rise," he said, "along with the other one."

"Other one?"

"The one that poor son of a bitch Baker was riding. I found Baker, by the way. His skull was bashed in. Did you do that, Maudie?"

"No," she said. "I didn't, and I'm sorry to hear about it. We decided to split up last night."

"Yeah?" He didn't believe her, but he decided not to pursue the subject.

"What are you doing out here?" she said.

Slocum had by this time walked around to stand facing Maudie. She still sat, still sipped her coffee. She seemed very calm, almost too calm.

"Didn't you know I'd come after you?"

"For what?"

"Don't play games with me, Maudie. We know you hired Giddings and them other two men. We know you paid to have all those men killed and them two fires started. We know all about the railroad. The game's up, ole gal. You're headed for jail, or a hanging."

Maudie shivered, but she got control of herself quickly.

"Well, why don't you sit down and have a cup of coffee?" she said. "The food will be ready in just a minute, too. No sense in riding off and leaving it, is there?"

She reached out to stir some beans. Slocum watched her carefully. He still did not know exactly what had happened to Baker, but he sure did not believe what Maudie had said. Maudie could be dangerous, and he knew it. He stepped in closer to the fire and sat down across from her.

"You can put that gun away," she said. "You can see I'm not armed. Even if I was, I wouldn't have a chance against a gunfighter like you. I guess you killed Giddings."

"I sure did."

Maudie gave a shrug. "He was my last chance, I guess. I was sure counting on that man."

"I bet you were," said Slocum.

Slocum holstered his Colt and reached for the cup of coffee she had poured for him. He sipped it, and it tasted good. He thought that this was likely to be the last of Maudie's coffee he would drink. He caught himself wondering what the other eating place in Guadalupe was like. Maudie began to spoon out the food onto two plates, and she handed one to Slocum.

"Well," he said, "thank you."

"My pleasure," she said. "Nothing like a last meal between old friends."

"It's good," he said, "but I'm not surprised about that. I always knew you could cook."

"I can do other things, too," she said, giving him a knowing look and a smile.

"Yeah," he said. "You sure can."

"Slocum," she said, between bites, "you don't have to take me back to Guadalupe. You could go away with me. I have a little money, and—"

"You have some of Baker's money, too, don't you?" he said, interrupting her.

"Yeah. I took it," she said. I didn't figure he'd be needing it. What do you say? You're no real lawman. You and I both know that."

"You tried to have me killed, Maudie," he said. "Twice."

"The situation was different then," she said coolly. "I didn't have any choice."

"You've always got a choice."

"What about now?"

"You already made your choice," he said. "You don't get a second chance."

They finished eating and Maudie cleaned up the dishes as before, with sand. Slocum helped her pack things up, and he put out the fire.

"Let's go," he said. "We got a long ride ahead of us."

She walked up close to him and put her arms around his shoulders, pressing her body up against his. It felt good. Slocum put his arms around her and squeezed her tight.

"Let's do take a long ride together. Away from Guadalupe. We could be good together," she said. "Remember?"

"I remember," he said, "and you sure are tempting, but I couldn't live with it. You've done too much." He pushed her away. "Get on your horse," he said.

"All right," she said with a shrug. "You had your chance. It's like you told me. You always have a choice. You just made the wrong one."

"We'll see about that."

She walked over to her horse's side and prepared to mount up. Slocum took the horse's reins. As Slocum turned his back to lead the horse up the hillside, Maudie slipped a hand into the saddlebags and came out with her Webley. She climbed into the saddle. Slocum started to walk up the hillside toward where he had left his Appaloosa and the other horse. Maudie slowly lifted the Webley to point it between his shoulder blades, and she thumbed back the hammer. Slocum heard the telltale click, and he made a dive. Maudie's shot tore flesh from his right shoulder. He hit the ground rolling and pulled out his Colt. He fired once, his shot knocking Maudie out of the saddle. He got up quickly and ran to her side. The Webley had fallen free. He knelt by her, and she opened her eyes to look at him.

"You had your chance," she said.

"Maudie," he said, "that was no chance at all."

Her eyes closed, and she was dead. Slocum stood up and took off his hat. He looked at the body of the beautiful woman lying there at his feet, and he looked up and away, wiping his forehead with his sleeve. What a waste, he thought. What a goddamn sorry waste. He picked up the once beautiful body and slung it across the saddle. Then he started walking up the hill. He would get his Appaloosa and the other horse and head back for Guadalupe. Along the way, he would stop and load up what was left of Baker. He figured that Holbrook would want something other than his word that he had stopped the two. Damn it, but this was a distasteful job.

•   •   •

When Slocum at last rode back into Guadalupe, he stopped first
in front of Riley's undertaking establishment. Riley came out in
a minute and looked at the two horses with the two bodies across
them. One was a woman. The other one, a fat man, was already
a little rank. Slocum thought that he could see money in the
man's eyes.

"Who you got there?" Riley asked.

"You'll recognize them," said Slocum.

"Send the bill to the sheriff's office?" Riley asked.

"Yeah," said Slocum. "Like usual. Take the horses back to
the stable when you're done with them. Will you?"

"Sure thing," Riley said.

He rode on, glad to be riding away from that scene. He was
sick of dropping off corpses for Riley to plant. He took his
Appaloosa to the stable. The big horse had earned some good
oats and a rest. He left it there with the man, telling him also
about his two horses that would shortly be returned to him, and
then he walked to the sheriff's office. He found the door unlocked, as usual, and went inside, but the place was deserted.
He walked back outside and stood on the sidewalk for a moment, wondering where to look for Holbrook. He caught himself
thinking for a second that he could walk over to Maudie's and
check there. Old habits die hard. It was late enough. He might
find the sheriff at the Hogback. He walked on over there and
went inside. There were few customers in the place. He did not
see Holbrook. He bellied up to the bar and ordered a drink of
whiskey. Amos brought it to him, and he paid for it. Then he
picked up the glass and drank it down fast. He ordered a second
and paid for that. This time he sipped at the brew. It was good.
It burned its way down to his stomach. He had needed it.

"Amos," he said.

"Another one?" Amos asked.

"No," Slocum said. "Do you know where Cy is at?"

"Why, I thought everyone knew that," said Amos.

"Well, I don't know," Slocum said. "If I did I wouldn't have
asked you. I been out of town. Will you tell me where the hell
I can find him?"

"Well, sure," said Amos. "He's down at the church. At least, as far as I know they're still down there."

Slocum downed the rest of his drink. "Thanks," he said, and he suppressed an urge to ask Amos what the hell Cy was doing at the church and who the hell "they" were. He turned to walk out of the place. He felt disgusted with the whole world. Outside, he stood for a moment looking down toward the church. There were a few horses and a buggy out in front of the place. He took a deep breath and started walking toward them. He almost wished he had kept the Appaloosa a little longer. The church was at the far end of town. He had never before had occasion to go that way. A church. What the hell was Holbrook doing down there? He passed a couple of cowhands on the way and greeted them in passing, but his greetings were none too friendly. When he reached the church, he mounted the stairs. He paused for a moment, feeling a little strange. Opening the door, he stopped, astonished. There was a goddamned wedding in progress. No mistake about that. He was looking at the backs of everyone, so it took him a moment to realize that the two folks being hitched up together were Cy Holbrook and Josie Yates.

"I'll be god damned," he said, fortunately in a very low voice. No one heard him. He walked in and shut the door behind himself very quietly. Then he sat down in the back pew, taking his hat off. He sat quietly while the wedding vows were being read by the preacher. Slowly but surely all the pain and the ugliness of the past weeks left him. The wedding was the beginning of a new life for Cy and Josie. The air suddenly felt fresher and cleaner than it had for a long time.

Watch for

SLOCUM AND THE HANGMAN'S LADY

308th novel in the exciting SLOCUM
series from Jove

Coming in October!